HALLEY HARPER,
SCIENCE GIRL EXTRAORDINAIRE:
SUMMER SET IN MOTION
BOOK 1

HALLEY HARPER
SCIENCE GIRL EXTRAORDINAIRE

SUMMER SET IN MOTION

TRACY BORGMEYER

ILLUSTRATED BY
MELANIE CORDAN

Tandem Services Press
GRAND RAPIDS, MICHIGAN

Copyright

ISBN 978-1-7325285-0-5

Library of Congress Control Number: 2018910543

Seuss, Dr. *Bartholomew and the Oobleck*. New York: Random House, 1949. Print.

To my favorite scientists: Allie, Andrew, and Avery

"An object in motion tends to remain in motion."
– Sir Isaac Newton

TABLE OF CONTENTS

Chapter 1: A Silly Solid   9

Chapter 2: A Missed Warning   15

Chapter 3: A Pantry Spy   19

Chapter 4: Miss Disaster   23

Chapter 5: Newton's Cradle   29

Chapter 6: Fish out of Water   37

Chapter 7: Team Trouble   45

Chapter 8: Operation Science Revenge   49

Chapter 9: Houston, We Have a Problem   55

Chapter 10: The Unbalanced Rock   67

Chapter 11: Brains are in Motion   73

Chapter 12: Lefty Loosey   83

Chapter 13: Science Girl Extraordinaire   87

Chapter 14: Friction Stops Motion   91

Chapter 15: Science Supply Jackpot   95

Chapter 16: A Diversion   101

Chapter 17: Campfire Confession   105

Chapter 18: Ms. Mac's Hangout   111

Chapter 19: The Cornstarch Project   117

Chapter 20: Team Comet's Contribution   121

Chapter 21: The Ride Home   125

Halley Harper: Science Girl Extraordinaire
    Book 2 Preview   127

Acknowledgments   133

About the Author   135

Glossary   136

Science Experiments in Summer Set in
    Motion   138

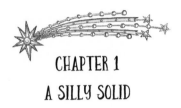

CHAPTER 1
A SILLY SOLID

AACHOOO!

Halley Harper sneezed right into her science experiment, blowing cornstarch dust all over the kitchen.

Some of the dust hung in midair before slowly settling on the clean, lemon-scented countertops. Dust was everywhere, even on the scratchy pink ballet costume Halley was wearing.

"Oopsie," Halley whispered, rubbing the end of her nose. "Well, I guess I don't need that much cornstarch." She looked around. Mom was going to kill her if she caught her with this mess; she had to hurry. She swept the dust off her favorite magazine, *Empower with Science*, and continued reading "How to Make your Own **Oobleck**."

"Make your own Non-Newtonian solid liquefy

before your very eyes! All you need are two ingredients: 2 cups cornstarch and 1 cup water. Add food coloring to make it your favorite color!"

She glanced over at the little, powdery cornstarch mountains in the shiny metal bowl. This was going to be so much cooler than the last potion she made! She reached for a measuring cup, filled it up with water from the sink, and carefully placed it next to the bowl. Maybe she should read the rest of the instructions before she poured it in.

"WARNING," Halley continued reading, "Do not—" and as if on cue, her four-year-old brother came roaring into the kitchen, slamming right into Halley.

"Hey Halley, whatcha doing?" Her little brother, Ben, traced big circles with his finger on the white, dusty counters. He was dressed in his favorite fireman costume.

"Ben, be quiet!" Halley snapped. "Stop making more of a mess. I'm going to clean up before Mom comes downstairs."

"What is this?" Ben said in his naturally loud voice, reaching for the bowl.

"Don't say anything to Mom, and you can watch me do a science experiment with icky, sticky goo." Halley said.

"Hooray science!" Ben shouted, tossing his fireman coat on the floor and jumping up and down. He was so excited that he bumped the cup of water, and it nearly fell off the counter.

"Calm down!" Halley shouted then regretted being so loud. "Wait until I tell you to pour it. You don't want to ruin the icky stickiness, do you?"

"Halley! What are you doing down there?" Mom called from upstairs. "Don't make a mess, okay? And don't forget to hang up your dance consume."

"Okay, Mom, we're just playing!" Halley called sweetly. Secretly, she wished Mom would just come down and do science with them. It was Halley's favorite thing in the whole entire world. Mom's favorite thing was not making a mess.

The instructions continued. "Add water and a few food coloring drops. Then slowly stir the cornstarch."

"Ben, you pour the water, and I'll stir." Halley squirted in a few drops of red food coloring and grabbed the wooden spoon.

At first, the powder and water was easy to stir and the food coloring formed pretty swirls in the cornstarch. Then it became harder to stir as it turned into a crumbly, liquid, pink mixture.

"Awesome!" Halley could not resist reaching down to touch the Oobleck with her finger. She tossed the spoon in the sink next to her and put both hands down into the bowl squishing and mixing it. "Wow, this feels dry and wet at the same time!" In all of her nine years, she had never done a cooler science experiment than this!

"Let me see! Let me see!" Ben reached for the bowl. "I want to touch the goo too!" Ben yanked the bowl from Halley's hand. The bowl slipped and crashed on the floor but the Oobleck didn't budge.

"Ben, geez, calm down!" Halley sat on the kitchen floor.

Ben joined her on the kitchen floor, and they put their hands in the bowl together. They took turns admiring the goo that dripped down like liquid.

Halley formed the Oobleck into a ball, laid it flat on her hand, and watched while it liquefied and oozed back into the bowl again. "Wow, it can be a solid and a liquid at the same time!"

"Ooooh… monster boogers." Ben pulled out his hands dripping and oozing with pink goo. He shoved his hand in Halley's face, pretending to smear it on her. "I want to get this stuff off my hands now!"

"Stop it! I'll help you in just a minute!" Halley reached up for the science magazine and tried to flip the pages with her messy hands.

The pages kept getting stuck, and Halley, without thinking, wiped her hands on her tutu. "Hey, how cool would it be to dance on this stuff?" She imagined dancing on top of the Oobleck at her dance recital.

"Now it's time for me to teach you the science behind this amazing fluid." Halley said in her best teacher voice. "Cornstarch mixed with water is a **Non-Newtonian fluid**. This means it doesn't behave like most fluids. It can be sticky and smooth and liquid and solid at the same time!" She looked up to make sure Ben was paying attention. "It's a silly solid! Isn't that funny?"

But somehow Ben managed to get the Oobleck in his hair and was slicking it up into a pink gooey mohawk sticking straight off his head. "Hey, I've got rock-and-roll hair!" he shouted.

"Oh no!" Halley reached for a dishtowel and tossed it on top of Ben's head. "I think it's time to clean up!"

"Hey… Mommy! Look at my rock-and-roll hair!" Ben pulled the dishtowel off his head.

Halley covered his mouth with her gooey hand.

"Shhh! Quiet, Ben!"

The gooey hand over his mouth startled him, and he started screaming even louder.

Then Halley heard Mom's footsteps coming down the stairs.

Halley tried to flatten Ben's hair and wipe the Oobleck out, but it was just making it worse.

"What are you guys doing down there? Ben, what are you saying about your hair?"

Mom's footsteps were coming faster. "You better not be making a mess! We just cleaned that kitchen."

Halley looked around. Pink Oobleck was oozing off the counters onto the floor. The kitchen already looked like a white dust tornado had hit.

Halley grabbed the bowl, turned on the water from the sink full blast, and started dumping Oobleck down as fast as she could. "We're not making a mess, Mom. I promise." Halley called. But the Oobleck was in no hurry to get out of the bowl. She started shaking the bowl while clawing at it with her fingernails.

Some of the Oobleck crumbled out of the bowl and started oozing down the drain. The sink made a glug glug noise and started filling up with pink water.

Halley reached for the garbage disposal and flipped the switch.

Zzzzzzz was all she heard. She'd really done it now.

Her mom reached the bottom step with a horrified look on her face.

Halley gulped.

CHAPTER 2
A MISSED WARNING

MOM GASPED. "HALLEY EDISON HARPER, what did you do?" The water was still running in the sink, and the garbage disposal sounded like a sick cat. When the sink started overflowing, Mom dashed to turn the water off. Water sloshed over the side.

Ben ran over to the sink and slipped down making a thud on the hard floor. He started to cry.

All of the different noises were too intense for Halley, and she put her hands over her ears to drown them out.

She carefully slid over and helped Ben up. She looked back and thought the water was almost the same color pink as her ballet costume.

Mom's face, on the other hand, was bright red, and she looked like steam could shoot out her ears, just like in the movies. Oh boy, she hadn't seen Mom this mad since making a bubbly soap volcano.

"What a complete disaster, Halley. What is this stuff anyways?" Mom picked up the science magazine with her two fingers. It, too, had not escaped the Oobleck disaster.

"Mom, it's a science experiment!" Halley explained. "It's Oobleck, a Non-Newtonian fluid!" But she could tell Mom really didn't want an answer unless it involved magically cleaning up the mess.

"Did you happen to read this part?" Mom reached over to flip the garbage disposal on and off a few times. "Warning: Do NOT pour this experiment down the drain. It will plug up the drain and cause damage."

"Oooh. Halley's in trouble!" Ben announced, clearly forgetting how Halley allowed him to play with her.

"You're not helping, Ben!" Halley screamed, grabbing for a roll of paper towels. "I'll clean this up, Mom, promise."

"I don't know, Halley; you've really gone and done it this time. What a complete disaster. And look at your costume! Your dance recital is tomorrow!" Mom reached down and touched Halley's limp ballet tutu glued together with Oobleck. "I don't even know where to start, but I know I'm going to have to get a plumber out here. For now, go outside. I'll just have to hose you two off. What a mess."

Halley and Ben walked out of the kitchen and opened the door to the backyard. She started thinking of all the ways Mom was going to punish her for this one while they waited by the garden hose. Maybe

Mom would ground Halley from seeing her best friend, Gracelyn? Maybe she wouldn't dance in her dance recital? Maybe she'd have to clean all the toilets in the house? Halley kept imagining the worst possible scenarios until Mom came outside.

"Okay, the plumber is on his way." Mom muttered, stepping off the porch. "Ben, you're first to get hosed off." Ben skipped up to Mom while she hosed down his hair. He danced in the water like a duck; He wasn't going to get punished.

"Listen, Halley, I love that you like science, I really do, but these disasters need to stop." Mom started carefully hosing off Halley's costume.

"Miss Disaster...Miss Disaster." Ben chanted in the background.

"You really must get this from your dad's side of the family because you certainly don't get it from me." Mom said. "I'm ready for all of your experimenting to stop here at the house and get it out of your system somewhere else."

"But Mom..." Halley pleaded "Everything I do isn't exactly a disaster. I just love creating new inventions and finding out new things. Next time, I'll do the Oobleck outside in my treelab with the rest of my experiments." She looked at her playhouse in the backyard. That would be a good compromise.

"Next time? I don't think there will be a next time." Mom snapped. "I'm also considering cancelling your subscription to *Empower With Science*. So far, it's just empowered you to make complete messes of our home."

"But that was a gift from Grandma!" Halley cried,

looking down at her hands. "How could you possibly keep me from doing science?" She decided right there that she needed to talk to Gracelyn. She would know how to cheer Halley up.

The Oobleck was no longer a silly solid as it oozed down Halley's hands and into pink streams through the flowerbed. She wondered if she'd ever get to make Oobleck again.

CHAPTER 3
A PANTRY SPY

THE SINK WAS REALLY CLOGGED up, almost beyond repair. The plumber worked and worked for over an hour, mumbling about kids and parents who don't watch them close enough. Meanwhile, Mom was in the kitchen pantry beginning her purge of anything related to kitchen science. The remaining orange boxes of cornstarch were the first to go then the vinegar, baking soda, food coloring, and even dish soap!

Halley's stomach growled while she watched all of this from the upstairs banister. She grabbed her stomach and realized that she hadn't eaten since before ballet. She decided to slip quietly downstairs, while Mom was paying the plumber, to raid the pantry for a snack.

Before she could reach for the bottom of the stairs, she heard a loud Brrrriiing!

Halley hopped inside the pantry and shut the door before Mom walked back into the kitchen to grab her phone. Surely she could hide in here and sneak something sweet to eat. Never mind that she was a bit claustrophobic. She wouldn't be in the pantry for long.

"Hello?" Mom sang into the phone. She must be happy now that the mess was cleaned and the science trash would be taken out. "Dee! How are you? Why, yes, you saw a plumber at our house. Thanks for checking; everything is fine!"

Halley was so glad that Mom's best friend was her best friend's mom. The one and only thing she guessed they had in common. Best friends. Maybe Ms. Dee could convince Mom not to banish science in the house forever and talk some sense into her.

Halley's stomach grumbled impatiently, so she reached for a fruit snack and tore open the package.

"Yes, Halley did it again." Mom's voice lowered. "This time it really was a disaster, and I've got to do something about her."

Halley strained to hear through the closed pantry door what Mom was saying. Halley looked around, grabbed a glass, and hoped a spy trick she saw in her science magazine worked. She remembered it said, "Sound is created by vibration, and a glass isolates the sound, helping you hear through walls!" Halley slumped to the floor, and pressed the glass up against the door while pressing her ears to the bottom of the glass. She squinted her eyes and strained to hear any hint of what was going to happen to her and her precious science experiments.

"This really is the last straw. I can't believe how

that stuff stopped up the sink. The last time she did something like this I had bubbles spewing out of a clay volcano ruining my kitchen table. I just have such a hard time understanding her."

"Wow." Halley looked down at the glass surprised. "This really does work. See, science can even help you eavesdrop on your mom!" She secretly wished Ms. Dee would stand up for her and be on her side. Dad would also protest ridding the house of science. He would have loved the Oobleck before it went down the sink!

"I know." Mom continued. "But where do you send a square peg in a round hole? I want her to be curious and smart, but she really needs to give up this nonsense and mess if she ever wants to fit in. Why can't she just be a normal little girl?"

Halley felt a rush of heat go up her neck to her ears and in her eyes. Did Mom just say she didn't fit in? Tears formed, and Halley wiped her eyes, feeling ashamed and embarrassed that her own mother was talking about her this way. Who did she want Halley to be like, anyways?

Mom's voice started fading. "Well, I need to channel her energy somewhere before she drives me absolutely crazy. I think this will be the perfect place."

What's the perfect place? Halley strained to hear. Mom must have walked into another room. Where was she going to send me? She put the glass down and started popping her fingers nervously.

She heard a noise and picked the glass back up to hear more of her mother's conversation. But suddenly, the pantry door opened and Halley fell out landing on the floor still holding the glass.

"Hey! What are you doing here, miss?"

Startled, Halley lifted her head from the kitchen floor. Great. Her own mother thought she didn't fit in, and now she'd been discovered as a spy.

CHAPTER 4
MISS DISASTER

WHO ARE YOU SPYING ON, kiddo?" Dad smiled as he held open the pantry door. He reached out to help her off the floor.

"I'm not spying! Who says I'm spying?" Halley sheepishly hid the glass behind her back. "I was just going to get a drink of water."

Dad had his hands on his hip, waiting for Halley to answer.

"Okay look, Dad. I've really done it this time. Promise you won't get mad at me?" She pleaded, hoping Dad would understand her side of the story. "I was just trying out another science experiment and things got a little, well, out of hand."

"Oh! Miss Disaster strikes again," Dad teased, calling her his pet name.

"Dad!" She sighed with a smile, secretly loving

when he teased her. "Mom is furious with me."

"Well, what was it this time? A revisit of an old experiment? What variable did you change this time? More soap in your soap volcano eruption? A sponge to aid in sopping up a kitchen oil spill? Better fizz for your fizzy soda explosion? I mean, really, what does your mother expect? We did name you after **Halley's Comet** after all!"

She beamed, very proud of her famous namesake. Then she remembered how Mom called her a square peg. Maybe if Mom could, she'd time travel back in time and change Halley's name, or worse, not want to be her mother at all!

"Remember the last time we talked about this, Halley?" Dad said. "I told you to keep your science outside in your treelab playhouse. That's why I built it for you."

"I know, Dad, but I really didn't think it would be that sticky, and it's so stinking hot outside!" Halley pleaded. The temperature in the Texas heat was really unbearable at times. "I especially didn't know it would totally clog up the sink."

"The sink?" Dad sighed as he pushed up his sleeves, getting ready for a messy repair.

"Daddy's home!" Ben screamed and, with crusty, dried leftover Oobleck in his hair, ran full blast towards Dad, giving him a hug.

Halley gave a little smile and was thankful for the interruption. "I think I'm going to head out to my treelab, Dad." She whispered so Ben couldn't hear. She thought it would be best to not be in sight when Mom told Dad about the disaster. Halley also just wanted to be alone. She turned and walked briskly away from her dad and brother.

The hot Texas sun had passed behind a cloud. A breeze blew gently through the huge oak tree that Halley's treelab was nestled in. From the outside, it looked like an ordinary playhouse.

Halley breathed in the outside air and started climbing the ladder. She stopped for a moment on the little porch at the top before going inside. She forgot all about the chaos earlier in the day. This was her happy place.

She pushed open the door and heard a loud popping noise. She yelped, realizing that she wasn't alone!

"Stop right there!" A petite, curly-headed girl blowing chewing gum bubbles and sitting cross legged shouted in an army-general voice. "What's the secret password?"

Halley knew in an instant who it was. "Gracelyn! How did you get here?" She must have been really upset to miss Gracelyn's rainbow-tasseled bicycle parked in her backyard. Gracelyn always turned ordinary things, like bikes, into something more colorful, glittery, and magical.

"No more questions. Password, please?" Gracelyn peered over her sunglasses, blew another bubble in her gum, and twisted her hair. She threatened to close the treelab door.

"Oh alright!" Halley sighed. "**Lefty loosey, righty tighty**!" She still thought it was a great password when Dad explained how to tighten the screws in her treelab.

Gracelyn held open the door for Halley before she closed it tight.

Halley plopped down on a bean bag chair in the corner of her treelab and inspected the inside. On the shelves were rows of old science experiment books her dad had given her. A few of them were his as a kid. She saw the balloon rockets still tied with string that her and Gracelyn had experimented with a few days earlier. On the wooden floor was an old rainbow colored carpet Gracelyn donated to the lab where Halley liked to sit and write poetry. Her favorite poetry was haiku because it involved numbers. Five syllables in one line, seven syllables in the next, and back to five again. Like an equation with words.

"What happened today? My mom sent me here to talk to you. She said your mom was furious. And by the way, I'm furious you didn't invite me over to do science before you dumped it down the drain!"

If Gracelyn knew Halley's experiment went down the drain, did she know that Halley's mom was banning science in their house? "Can we just stop talking about it? Mom's pretty mad, and I'm not sure what I'm going to do." Halley ran her fingers over her telescope, still positioned to see the Big Dipper. What should she do inside the treelab? Looking at the boxes, string, and tape lying on the floor, about to be made into an amazing invention, Halley wished that she was more organized.

"Well, you are never going to believe the surprise I have for you!" Gracelyn squealed. "This really is the best news ever! Close your eyes and put out your hands."

"Gracelyn, I'm in no mood for games." Halley said, rolling her eyes. "but just this once because you're my best friend." She held out her hand and squeezed her eyes tight.

A roll of paper landed in her hand. "Can I open my eyes now, Goofball?"

"We're going to summer camp together!" Gracelyn shouted before Halley could figure it out herself.

"What? A summer camp?" Halley unrolled the camp flyer. "A sleep-away camp at Camp... Eureka? What the heck is Camp Eureka?"

"You are going to love it, Halley!'" Gracelyn said. "Mom's been looking for a camp to send me to when school lets out this summer. When our moms were talking earlier, they decided to sign us up!"

Halley looked back down at the camp flyer with a big light bulb and the words Eureka! peering back at her. A sleep-away camp sounded pretty amazing right now.

Camp Eureka
"Summer Set in Motion"
Join us for experiments, teamwork, and fun!
A Note to Parents: Camp is a per-
fect way to keep the mess at camp while
bringing home an inquiring mind.

Halley smirked when she read the note to parents and was certain that it convinced her mom to sign her up. "Gracelyn, this does look amazing. But my mom is banning science for good here at the house. If I go away to camp, it will be like caving in to her and only doing fun experiments at this camp. I've got to think of a way to convince Mom that I can be more responsible."

"What!? No, your mom was just mad. She'll chill out when you get back from camp and show her all the cool stuff we'll do! I've already started packing! This is going to be so much fun! Our first sleep-away camp together."

"I guess you're right." Halley folded the flyer into a quick paper airplane and chucked it toward Gracelyn. "Camp Eureka does look fun. We can stay up late telling ghost stories and eating junk food!"

The sound of the back door opening caused her to suddenly stop daydreaming.

"Halley, it's time for dinner." Mom shouted outside.

"Gotta go!" Gracelyn scurried down the ladder and got on her bike. "See you soon!" She pedaled toward home.

"Clean up the playhouse, come inside, and start packing your bags. After your dance recital tomorrow, you are heading to camp. Mommy's cleaning house."

Halley looked down at Mom holding a garbage bag then up at her homemade sign above her treelab window: For every action there is an equal and opposite reaction.

Wasn't that the truth. With Halley at science camp, Mom could chuck all her science inventions at home. Ironic!

CHAPTER 5
NEWTON'S CRADLE

A BUZZ FILLED THE PERFORMANCE HALL and colorful, costumed dancers flitted backstage. The bright lights shone down on the stage and fifteen pink ballerinas kicked up bits of feather, glitter, and sequins as they ran to their starting positions. Suddenly, the curtains were pulled back and the Under the Stars recital began.

Halley had practiced this dance so many times that she didn't even have to think; her muscles already knew what to do. That's what she loved about dancing; she could just focus on the music and nothing else. Not the audience, not her scratchy ballet costume, not her mom, and not Camp Eureka. All she had to think about now was remembering to smile.

When the music started, Halley twirled, leaped, and sashayed through the performance grinning from ear to ear. She didn't even mind that her costume was crusty with cornstarch and her tutu was deflated from being hosed off with a water hose. Tonight she was the star of the show. Tomorrow she would be another camper at Camp Eureka.

That night Halley packed her suitcase and favorite red backpack full of rations she thought she would need for camp. The next morning she stood by the front door waiting for her ride and admiring the bright red bouquet of roses that Ben and her Dad had given her for her ballet performance. She wondered what they would look like when she got home after a week of camp.

Honk Honk! A Volkswagen beetle bumped into Halley's driveway, and a curly headed girl bounced up and down in the backseat. Gracelyn must have insisted that Ms. Dee lay on the horn to alert Halley that they were there to pick her up for camp.

She took a deep breath and reached for the doorknob.

"Not so fast there, Miss Disaster," her Dad said, smiling as he put his arm across the door. He looked out the side windows and motioned to Ms. Dee to wait a minute. "You forgot to put this in your suitcase." He held out a colorful bound book and a pen.

"Dad... what is this?" Halley took the notebook and held it tenderly. She flipped through the pages with her thumb. They were empty. "What kind of book is this?"

"Let me explain," Dad said. "I noticed there is a writing contest in your *Empower With Science* magazine for the best article explaining what summer science means to you. I thought you could use this to take notes about what you learn at your first sleep away camp." Halley's Dad smiled, waiting for her reaction. "Besides, I'm kind of curious myself what you'll learn at this camp."

"Dad, this is so sweet. Thank you." Halley beamed looking down at the notebook. "I promise I'll take good notes for you."

Dad lifted her suitcase and headed outside to load it into Ms. Dee's car. He opened the car door for Halley to get in. "Have a safe trip and have fun!"

"Tell Mom and Ben bye for me," Halley said before Dad softly closed the door behind her.

"Woohoo!" Gracelyn screamed. "Summer camp, here we come!" Ms. Dee peeled out of the driveway, honking her horn as they went down the street.

Halley smiled and looked back out the rear window. Dad was standing there waving. She carefully put her notebook in her red backpack. She was going to miss him for sure. She turned back around. "How long is it before we get there?"

"Oh, it's a good two-hour drive," Ms. Dee said. "But don't worry. We'll stop for a snack before we get there."

"Aren't you excited, Halley?" Gracelyn said, looking over at her. "Hey, are you okay? You look like someone ran over your cat! Did we run over your cat?"

"No, silly. Atom the Cat is just fine. I guess I'm just a little sad." Halley swallowed a catch in her throat. She regretted saying it so loud that Ms. Dee would hear. Ms. Dee probably already felt sorry for Halley after her mom called her weird.

"Sad! What could you possibly be sad about?" Gracelyn questioned, putting her hand on Halley's shoulder.

"Gracelyn…" Ms. Dee cautioned, glancing in the rearview mirror. "Halley, look, you are heading to your first sleep-away camp. You are probably feeling a bit homesick, but you're going to love it there. Who knows? You girls just might meet some new, interesting friends!"

Halley agreed. She stared out the car window as they turned out of her neighborhood and merged onto the busy Houston highway heading to the piney Texas woods.

"It's okay, Halley, I'm going to be there," Gracelyn said. "And think about it this way. We both get exactly what we love! You get science, and I get to hang out with you!"

Halley looked over at her best friend. She just loved how excited Gracelyn was. Not just about going to camp but about life in general. Gracelyn was always a bundle of sunshine. That's what Halley loved about her.

"Come on, Halley! You always love an adventure. What an amazing one this will be!" She bounced a little, constrained by her seatbelt. "Hey, I know, let's play the license plate game!"

Ms. Dee turned on some retro 80s music, "Girls Just Want to Have Fun," and opened the car's sunroof.

Instantly, Halley's heart lightened, and they sang at the top of their lungs. Car games made the trip go by so fast. When Ms. Dee turned the car left, Halley and Gracelyn dramatically fell on each other to the right. When she turned to the right, they giggled and fell on each other to the left. And they even found a rare Hawaii license plate in Texas!

They left the tall buildings of downtown Houston behind them and traveled north for what seemed like hours where the tall trees on either side of the highway made it feel like they were heading into a forest.

"Almost there, girls," Ms. Dee announced. "Gather up your things!"

Halley was the first to spot the green balloons marking the camp turnoff. Older kids were dressed in rainbow lab coats, mismatched sneakers, and white mad-scientist wigs. Some were holding signs that said, "Welcome Campers!" and "Eureka! You made it!" Others were holding bubbling beakers with green liquid in them.

The Volkswagen happily bumped into the main entrance under a giant wooden sign that read, "Welcome to Camp Eureka: Where we believe play is the highest form of research." Kids were milling around the cabins wearing the bright green camp shirts. Others were playing near a huge lake in the middle of camp.

"I think I'm really going to like it here." Halley unfolded her legs, pushed the car door open, and jumped out to stretch.

The summer sun was already becoming unbearably hot. They entered the main camp building and enjoyed a blast of air conditioning.

Tired of being stuck in the car, they decided to go exploring in the building while Ms. Dee checked them in.

"Wow, Halley!" Gracelyn gasped, and their voices

and footsteps echoed as they walked down a huge hallway. Pictures of past camp sessions showing suntanned kids smiling with their arms around each other's necks were tacked to the walls. What appeared to be past camp projects were lined up and down the hall.

One of the projects instantly caught Halley's attention as it sat motionless.

They ran over to the contraption and inspected the five golden balls the size of bowling balls, hanging from thick wires inside a frame.

"This is amazing!" Halley reached out and pushed the end bowling ball with her hand.

All the balls moved back and forth together like a pendulum. Then it stopped, once again motionless.

"I'm not sure we're supposed to touch it." Gracelyn looked around to see if anyone was watching them.

"Wait a minute." Halley scratched her head. "I've seen one of these at my grandma's house, but it was a lot smaller. Grandma called it a Newton's cradle. I used to love pulling back on the end ball and watching it strike the balls in the middle making the ball at the other end pop out. Then it goes back and forth like a pendulum until it loses energy and stops. I bet this is a ginormous **Newton's cradle**!"

"Maybe we should get back to check in." Gracelyn looked around, a frown on her face.

"Oh come on, Gracelyn. Don't be such a scaredy cat. Why would it be sitting here if we weren't supposed to touch it?" Halley picked up the end bowling ball, raising it above her head. "Now move back so you don't get bonked by the end ball popping up."

Halley let go of the end ball.

BAM! The Newton's cradle was in motion.

Halley came to stand next to Gracelyn in front of the cradle. They watched the balls pop out and back again while the middle balls stayed still.

CLACK! CLACK! CLACK! The back-and-forth motion mesmerized the girls.

"What do you two think you are doing?" A voice shouted as the giant Newton's cradle halted to a stop.

Halley gasped and turned around to face someone with only one eyebrow.

CHAPTER 6
FISH OUT OF WATER

DON'T YOU KNOW THAT CURIOSITY killed the cat?" A tiny lady with wild, frizzy hair stood smiling at them with her hands on her hips. She pushed one hand out to shake their hands. "Howdy, I'm Ms. Mac, the Camp Director. You must be Halley Harper. So nice to finally meet you."

It surprised Halley how firm Ms. Mac's handshake was for such a small lady.

"Uh, yes, and this is my best friend, Gracelyn. I'm sorry. Were we not supposed to touch this Newton's cradle?" Halley asked innocently.

"Oh well." Ms. Mac sighed, scratching where her eyebrow would have been. "No harm's done. This contraption can show you so many things. One is by lifting the ball you give it **potential energy**, or what I like to call stored energy, before you let it go. Then once they are in motion they have **kinetic energy**. But my absolute favorite is," Ms. Mac leaned in closer and whispered, "for every action there is an equal and opposite reaction." Ms. Mac stood back up taller and crossed her arms. "Now, you two run along and join the other campers playing volleyball before camp is in session."

"Thanks," the girls said in unison, thankful they didn't get in trouble. They turned and walked quickly down to the heavy metal doors at the end of the hallway.

"Whew, that was a close one!" Gracelyn whispered. "I told you not to touch it!"

Halley was lost in thought, wondering what happened to Ms. Mac's eyebrow. She looked back at Ms. Mac for a moment.

The wild-haired camp director was inspecting the Newton's cradle for a moment. Then she turned around as if to see if anyone was looking and grabbed one of the balls and let go. She stood there smiling and waving her arms like she was conducting an orchestra.

Halley turned and grabbed Gracelyn's hand, and they stepped into the blazing Texas heat and ran full blast towards the kids playing near the volleyball nets.

As they got closer, they realized they were the only girl campers playing outside.

"I wonder where the other girls are?" Gracelyn said, looking around.

"I'm not sure, but let's play. This looks like fun! It's water balloon volleyball!" Halley picked up a large towel and a water balloon. "You hold one end of the towel, I'll hold the other and don't let the water balloon break!"

They each held an end of the same towel and

balanced the water balloon in the middle. "See how the water balloon has potential energy inside the towel before it has kinetic energy by being tossed over the net?" Halley said to herself out loud.

"Let's not think about it too hard, Halley. Let's just go play!" Gracelyn said, giving the water balloon a bounce in the towel. They got into position directly opposite of two boys, one with wavy brown hair, and tossed the water balloon over to him and his partner.

"Ready to get soaked?" The boy grinned as he and his partner quickly tossed the water balloon back to Halley and Gracelyn.

"Hey, we weren't ready!" Halley said, running over to the water balloon and narrowly missing it. She tossed the water balloon a little too hard back in the boy's direction.

"Halley, take it easy. I wasn't ready." Gracelyn said.

"This kid is annoying," Halley barked back. "I refuse to get soaked by this jerk."

"See if you can catch this one!" They launched the return volley high above the net. The balloon made a beeline for Halley's head.

Halley side stepped with white knuckles hanging onto the towel, jerking Gracelyn her direction and barely catching the water balloon.

A few other campers had gathered and were watching the back and forth exchange.

The girls volleyed it back quicker than expected to the boys and the water balloon fell and busted at the boys' feet.

"Ooh... Nathan got beat by a girl!" Some of the onlookers pointed and covered their mouths. Still smirking, Nathan looked down at his feet and kicked the balloon pieces.

"Well, that was fun." Halley looked at Gracelyn and they gave each other high fives. "Come on. Let's go in and find something to drink."

They turned and walked away when suddenly something hit her on the back and exploded. Halley was jolted forward. And she was soaked.

Halley's face heated as she slowly turned to look for the culprit that had pelted her. Then she noticed in the distance that Ms. Mac was also coming towards them with another skinny lady whose lips curled as she sized up the wet camper standing before her.

"Well, don't you look like a fish out of water?" Ms. Mac chuckled. "Did you lose at water balloon volleyball, Halley?"

The other co-director, Ms. Spark, pushed up her thin wire-frame glasses, pursed her lips together, and pulled a Camp Eureka clipboard close to her.

"Yes, I guess we did." Halley peered over her shoulder at Nathan, the apparent balloon assailant. The other campers in the background were laughing at them.

A smirk played on Nathan's lips even though he was looking down, shifting from foot to foot.

Should Halley tell on him? "It's a hot day, so I decided to cool off a bit." Halley brushed pieces of water balloon off her shoulder.

"Water balloon fights are not camp protocol," Ms. Spark said slowly, while primly writing on her Camp Eureka clipboard. Even a sticker of Albert Einstein on her clipboard seemed to cringe as she etched her notes on the paper. "I expect campers to follow all camp protocol." Ms. Spark spoke through her nose.

"Oh, we'll worry about protocol after the camp kicks off, Ms. Spark." Ms. Mac said, patting Halley on the shoulder. "Well, boys, why don't you run along to Cabin Einstein. Girls, your bags are already at your Cabin Curie over yonder, so clean up and be back in 30 minutes to Energy Hall for camp kickoff before dinner. Run along now."

Gracelyn helped Halley wring out her ponytail as they sloshed towards Cabin Curie.

"Who pelted you with the water balloon?" Gracelyn finally broke the silence.

Halley turned and saw the rest of the boys peeling off from the crowd, but she locked eyes with Nathan. He was staring at her, smiling.

"I'm sure Nathan did, but don't worry, I've got an idea. He'll never mess with us girls again."

"Oh Halley, what do you have in mind? I don't want to get into trouble. That Spark lady looked like she meant business and would have no problem kicking us out of camp if we didn't follow the rules." Gracelyn protested. "Besides, I don't want to leave camp with only one eyebrow like Ms. Mac!" Gracelyn smiled, peering over at Halley while raising her eyebrows up and down.

"Gracelyn, quit goofing around. We've got a lot of work to do." Halley said as they reached Cabin Curie.

A sign outside the girl's cabin read, "Nothing in life is to be feared. It is only meant to be understood. – Marie Curie, scientist." They swung open the door to the dark cabin. The cabin was empty except for two wooden bunk beds.

"Well, it's not much, but it will do. We're really going to need to spruce up this place!" Gracelyn rubbed her hands together.

Halley started rummaging through her bags and tossed her sleeping bag with constellations on the top bunk. "I called dibs!" she said quickly.

"We both can have a top bunk because there are two bunk beds!" Gracelyn laughed while carefully spreading her unicorn sleeping bag on hers.

"Gracelyn, there's not much time. I'm going to need your help!" Halley tossed her a small bottle of glitter and a bag of balloons. "Fill 'em up!" Halley started shaking a can of shaving cream in one hand and holding her *Empower With Science* magazine in the other. "Science Practical Jokes," she read. "This will be perfect!"

"Um, okay." Gracelyn shook glitter into a balloon. "Do we really need the glitter?" She looked down. Her hands were covered in silvery flecks. She handed Halley the glitter balloon.

"It's for style points." Halley grinned, filling up the balloon with shaving cream. For a moment, Halley missed her dad because the cabin started smelling just like him shaving in the morning.

"What are you planning on doing with all of this, Miss Disaster?" Gracelyn joked, handing Halley another balloon laced with glitter.

"Oh, you know, just Operation Science Revenge. He'll never know what hit him." Halley tied off the balloons while peering out the window at the cabin next door.

Campers were coming out of Cabin Einstein and

heading towards Energy Hall. Nathan was the last to leave the cabin, carefully closing the door behind him.

"We've got to work fast." Halley loaded five shaving-cream balloons in her backpack. "It's going to take a little while to make the perfect booby trap." The girls snuck out their cabin door and headed toward Cabin Einstein.

CHAPTER 7

TEAM TROUBLE

THE CAMP KICKOFF WAS JUST about to begin
when Halley and Gracelyn rushed into Energy
Hall slightly out of breath. They had changed
into their bright green camp shirts and managed to
blend in with the other campers, finding a seat in the
front.

The room buzzed while the kids waited. There
was an excited energy in the air and most of the campers couldn't stay in their seats.

"Take your seat, campers. We will begin shortly!"
Ms. Mac announced over the loud speakers.

Halley scanned the crowd looking for Nathan.
"He can't suspect anything," Halley whispered to
Gracelyn.

He was sitting in the back talking to a few of his
cabin mates. He caught the girls watching him, and he

had an annoying grin on his face as he waved at them.

"Welcome to the Tenth Annual Session of Camp Eureka!" Ms. Mac sang out, taking the stage while holding a microphone in one hand and a clipboard in the other. Ms. Spark was sitting behind Ms. Mac and looked like she had better things to do. "We have a lot of exciting activities planned for you!" Ms. Mac said. "But first I want you to give a round of applause to the teen camp counselors that will be helping you this week."

The campers clapped awkwardly as the counselors stood and waved.

Halley clapped, noticing one of the counselors was a girl. At least they were not the only girls here. Halley vowed to introduce herself to the girl counselor. She thought being a counselor one day would be fun. Halley's stomach growled as they sat down. She was hungry!

"You will be working in teams of three this week on challenges related to Newton's Laws of Motion. Winners of each challenge will receive a coupon to the General Store to buy your favorite science treat. My favorite is color-changing Popsicles. Try it. You'll like it!" Ms. Mac grinned.

The campers started humming, talking about the General Store. Ms. Spark rolled her eyes and tapped her foot. She looked down and checked her watch.

"All right, campers, quiet down. Now, you will find your teams posted on the wall outside Energy Hall, so before you head to dinner make sure you take a look. Ms. Spark, our camp co-director, is going to give you the schedule and a few... uh, rules to remember.

Ms. Spark, take it away." Ms. Mac cleared her throat and shifted a bit uncomfortably. Ms. Spark ascended the stage and took the microphone as if it was covered in germs. She tapped on it, and it made a squealing sound.

The campers' energy shifted from laughing to holding their ears to complete silence.

Halley was excited about exploring the General Store and then got a sinking feeling that maybe she and Gracelyn wouldn't be on the same team.

"Thank you, Ms. Mac." Ms. Spark touched her head lightly, raised her eyebrows, and looked down at her camp clipboard. "I'm going to tell you the camp schedule and a few rules for your safety... not that you're going to follow them all," Ms. Spark said, partially under her breath. "According to the camp handbook, meals will be served promptly at Pie Are Square dining hall at 8 AM, noon, and 6 PM. In the unlikely event you are injured due to wildlife attack, heatstroke, or broken bones, you are to go to the medic to be treated."

Halley turned to Gracelyn and whispered, "Gee, it can't be that bad."

Gracelyn shrugged and turned back to Ms. Spark.

"You will have free time after meals, but campers are to promptly be in their cabins at 9 PM. If there are any questions, you can refer to your camp handbook that your parents signed. It is expected that you will follow these rules to the T or face consequences. Any questions?" Ms. Spark surveyed the room.

Crickets chirped somewhere, but no one else dared to speak.

"Okay, Ms. Spark, thank you." Ms. Mac took the microphone and cleared her throat. "Well, we don't want to be between you and dinner. Just remember, the two most important rules here at Camp Eureka is to have fun and discover science! Campers dismissed!"

The campers collectively breathed a sigh of relief and stood, shuffling their way toward dinner.

"Be sure to check your teams before you leave!" Ms. Mac said.

"Come on, Gracelyn. We've got to make sure we made it on the same team." Halley yanked Gracelyn toward the posted lists. She scanned the names. "Oh no, what were the chances?" Halley's stomach started to feel like she just ate soggy asparagus.

"Hey, team!" Nathan cheered, pushing his way towards the girls.

Halley was sure her face looked as green as the camp shirts they were wearing.

CHAPTER 8

OPERATION SCIENCE REVENGE

L OOK ON THE BRIGHT SIDE," Gracelyn said. "At least we are on a team together!"

Halley saw Ms. Spark walking in their direction. "Hey, maybe we could ask her to move Nathan off our team," Halley whispered to Gracelyn. "Um, excuse me. Ms. Spark?" Halley bounded up to Ms. Spark. "I think there has been a mistake. Can we submit a request to change teams?" Halley said, pretending to be braver than she felt.

Ms. Spark took a deep long breath, pushed up her glasses, and then stooped down to Halley's height holding a camp clipboard close to her chest. "It says here on page 32 of the camp handbook that all posted teams are final. You obviously did not read this handbook." Ms. Spark looked over the top of her glasses. "I suggest you do, Miss Harper."

Ms. Spark was so close, Halley could smell the old coffee on her breath like rotten mothballs.

"I don't see why you girls would want to come to this camp anyways. I'll be watching you very, very closely." Ms. Spark spoke slowly, as if talking to a small child. She straightened and walked off with her nose perched high in the air.

Halley stared straight ahead, stunned. She looked back at Gracelyn and Nathan standing next to one another, astonished at what just happened.

"Gee, tell us how you really feel, Ms. Spark," Nathan said.

Halley squinted at Nathan. She wished she could let out a growl.

"Hey, I know the perfect team name!" Nathan proposed. "What do you think of Halley's Comets?" Nathan paused then he busted out laughing.

Halley grabbed Gracelyn's hand and yanked her in the direction of Pie Are Square. "Come on, Gracelyn, let's get something to eat." They left Nathan behind as they raced off to the dining hall.

"We've got to hurry," Halley said. "I want a front-row seat to Operation Science Revenge. He really deserves it now." Halley looked at her hands and wiped at a bit of glittery evidence still on her fingers.

Halley and Gracelyn scarfed down their pizza and ran back to Cabin Curie. They turned the lights out and waited patiently for Nathan to come back to his cabin. They couldn't contain their giggles and kept shushing each other.

The other campers must have been enjoying several slices of pizza because no one came back to the boys' cabin for a long while.

"What if we get caught?" Gracelyn said.

"Oh, it's just a harmless camp prank. Besides, he deserves it for making fun of my name and embarrassing me with a water balloon," Halley said.

They waited for what seemed like forever, but the first person to come back to the boys' cabin was not Nathan.

"Uh oh!" Halley said under her breath. "What is she doing here?"

As Ms. Spark got closer to the cabin, the girls could hear her saying something about a first-night cabin check. Nathan followed close behind. "In light of all the pranks that were pulled last summer, Nathan Ryder, we felt it was best to check cabins to avoid that mess." Ms. Spark hurried towards the cabin.

"Wait!" Halley whispered, reaching her hand out.

Ms. Spark reached for the cabin knob and opened the door.

Halley winced in anticipation.

Ms. Spark opened the cabin door and triggered Operation Science Revenge intended for Nathan. One by one, shaving cream balloons busted right on top of Ms. Spark's head. She stood, stunned, while the balloons fell.

SPLAT! SPLAT! SPLAT! The balloons burst, sending shaving cream all over the cabin floor. Nathan side stepped each one, missing the shaving cream explosion.

Halley's jaw dropped. She waited for a reaction.

Gracelyn snorted under her breath as the balloons kept falling.

Halley looked at Gracelyn laughing and couldn't

help but start laughing too.

"Well, what goes up must come down," Halley said, smiling.

Ms. Spark stood with her arms out. Her glasses were crooked, and she still was clutching her Camp Eureka clipboard. "What is the meaning of this!" She clenched her fists, and then reached up to wipe shaving cream out of her hair.

"I swear, Ms. Spark, I had nothing to do with this. Look, it has glitter in it!" Nathan smirked, wiping his hand on his shirt.

"Clean this up, Nathan Ryder, or you will be severely punished." Ms. Spark sloshed off looking like a soggy, glittery, shaving-cream snowman.

"Operation Science Revenge!" Halley and Gracelyn gave each other high fives. "But why did I insist on adding glitter?" Halley questioned. "I hope she doesn't suspect us!"

"She deserved it," Gracelyn said.

The girls stepped onto their cabin porch with their hands on their hips, inspecting the aftermath.

"Hey, team!" Nathan grinned, shouting over to their cabin. "Was that meant for me? Because that was a good one!" He started to laugh, holding an empty can of shaving cream.

Hearing a shout, they looked to see Ms. Spark slipping down in the mud. Growling, she got back up.

"She's pretty mad." Nathan walked over to them. "But she deserved it for the girl comment she made earlier."

At that moment, Halley didn't mind that she and Gracelyn were the only girls at science camp. They were all there because they loved science, and she couldn't wait to start the challenges. She looked over at her two friends giggling at Ms. Spark. "Come on, let's clean this mess up."

They found a water hose nearby and started spraying the shaving cream. It ran in little white streams off the cabin porch.

That night, Halley lay wide awake in her top bunk. Thinking of all the things she saw that day, her brain just wouldn't turn off and let her go to sleep. She looked over to see if Gracelyn was awake and heard her snoring in the bunk across the room. She grabbed a flashlight and the diary her dad gave her and sat up in bed to start writing.

Monday
Dear Diary,

I like it here at Camp Eureka. So far, being the only girl campers hasn't been so bad. I'm glad Gracelyn is here. I'm going to try writing to you every day at camp so I don't forget what I've learned. Dad says I could get published in Empower Science Magazine*! Grandma will think that is so cool. So here it goes.*

Energy is everywhere. Something doesn't have to be moving to have energy. Energy can be stored depending on where it's located. Shaving cream balloons have stored energy when balancing over a door. Stored energy is also called potential energy.

Then when the shaving cream balloons are set in

motion, they have kinetic energy while they fall down...
SPLAT!!!

> *Love,*
> *Halley*

> *P.S. I have a teammate that has the potential to be a great friend too.*

CHAPTER 9

HOUSTON, WE HAVE A PROBLEM

A LOUD BIRD IN THE WOODS chirped like an alarm clock. A sunbeam shone through the windows of Cabin Curie right onto Halley's face.

Halley covered her head with her pillow to drown out the bird and rolled over, hoping to go back to sleep. For a moment, she forgot where she was. Then she saw her diary still open and looked over to see Gracelyn wrapped in her unicorn sleeping bag. Halley sat up in bed. Ack! The clock in the corner said 8:00! They overslept on the first day of camp!

"Gracelyn, wake up. We're going to be late!" Halley swung her legs over and jumped off the top bunk. She started looking frantically for her shoes and her backpack.

Gracelyn sat up, yawned, and scratched her head. "What happened to the alarm clock?"

"We've got to hurry!" Halley pulled her hair into a pony tail. She stuffed her red backpack with powdered donuts and bottled water. "There's no time for breakfast, let's head straight to Energy Hall."

"I've got no energy at all." Gracelyn rubbed her eyes and pulled on her rainbow tie-dyed shorts.

"Here, these will help." Halley tossed her some extra powdered donuts and was thankful that she had raided Mom's pantry for snacks before she left home.

Gracelyn caught them and continued applying sunscreen to her face and arms. "Halley, we don't want to get sunburn!" She pulled on her unicorn fanny pack. "I've got bug spray, Band-Aids, and bite cream. Oh and hand sanitizer!"

Halley looked at her and smiled. Her best friend was always prepared. She had a long streak of white sunscreen down her nose. "We've got to hurry, Gracelyn." Halley added to her backpack some fruit snacks and a few balloons. She never knew when those would come in handy.

They finally pushed open the cabin door and saw a counselor walking quickly towards them. She looked annoyed, tugging at her long red braid. When she got closer, the girls saw a sticker on her shirt that said, "Hi, I'm Cameron." She had freckles and a tan from the summer already.

Halley always wanted freckles.

"You guys are late. Hurry up! The first challenge is about to start by Lake Archimedes!" She scowled at her fellow girl campers.

"Sorry, we just overslept." Halley started to feel out of place with how over-prepared she and Gracelyn were. They both smelled like coconut sunscreen in the middle of a wooded forest. Cameron might realize that they were just city girls on their first camp trip. Being late probably didn't make a good first impression either.

"I told them that you guys shouldn't have a cabin all to yourselves. Nine-year-olds can be so irresponsible." Cameron rolled her eyes and then walked ahead of them, her braid swinging back and forth like a pendulum.

Halley and Gracelyn looked at each other and shrugged. As they walked, they tried to keep up with Cameron. The dust from the trail kicked up and stuck to their sun-screened legs. Cameron started slowing down the closer they got to the lake where the other campers were assembled.

The water in Lake Archimedes was calm and quiet. Halley smiled. She saw little ripples sparkling in the sun. Last summer, she swam in her grandma's pool, and she hoped they'd be able to swim in the lake while they were at camp. The morning felt humid, but the sun wasn't blazing down on them yet. Halley was sure it was going to be another hot Texas summer day. The girls found Nathan chatting with a few other boys. When Halley walked up, they quickly stopped talking to Nathan and left.

"What's wrong with them?" Halley asked.

"Well, the guys were making fun of me last night for being on a girl team, but I told them you'd pull a prank on them like you did to Ms. Spark and they stopped teasing me."

Ms. Mac saw the girls as they joined the crowd and said, "Some of us must have been burning the midnight oil! Ready to begin?"

A few campers giggled, and Halley was embarrassed. "I wonder if Ms. Spark told Ms. Mac about what happened last night," Halley whispered to Nathan and hoped that Ms. Mac hadn't labeled her and Gracelyn as trouble makers.

Ms. Mac stepped onto a small outdoor stage and stood behind a big table covered with a red-checkered tablecloth. The table was set with a glass pitcher of tea and several small glasses of ice. The table set up against the wooded forest looked as out of place as Ms. Spark did, sitting in a folding chair fanning herself with her clipboard.

"Good morning, Camp Eureka!" Ms. Mac sang out. We're learning all about Newton's Laws of Motion this week so beware, you don't want to be like **Sir Isaac Newton** and have an apple fall on your head!" Ms. Mac smirked and looked out of the corner of her eyes towards Ms. Spark. Ms. Spark rolled her eyes at the dig. One camper coughed and a few other campers were shifting their weight, anticipating Ms. Mac's challenge instructions.

"Okay, let's get started. It's all about objects at rest staying at rest. That's what this camp is all about, and once you start moving that's when the magic happens." And in one swift motion, Ms. Mac leaned down and yanked the tablecloth from the table like a magician. For a split second the crowd of campers gasped.

Ms. Mac stood wide eyed, one eyebrow raised with the red-checkered tablecloth in one hand. "Voila!" She stared at the glass and pitchers that remained motionless. Some of the campers started to clap.

"Whoa!" Halley said under her breath and looked over at Cameron who smiled, hands on her hips. She looked like she'd seen the trick before. Ms. Spark shifted, crossed her legs, and rolled her eyes at the corniness of the demonstration.

"And that, Campers, happened because of a fancy little word called **inertia**." Ms. Mac twirled the tablecloth around her arm. "The glasses wanted to stay at rest since gravity is pulling them down. I didn't make enough **friction** to overcome gravity so the glasses stayed put. The forces acting on these are balanced, the table pushing up on the glasses and the gravity pulling down on the glass. So the glasses don't move." The campers stared wide eyed.

"Now let's get you moving." Ms. Mac poured herself some tea into one of the unscathed glasses. "We're going to explore the beautiful woods around us looking for science. At the end of our journey, we will have a Newton's Laws of Motion challenge and a special time-honored Camp Eureka tradition for you."

And with that, Ms. Mac twirled around, jumped off the stage, and started walking into the woods. The campers followed her while Ms. Spark and the teen counselors trailed the campers from behind.

Halley had never really explored the woods before. The closest she got to this many trees was a bayou with a trail that her family would bicycle around occasionally. She was glad she wasn't alone in the woods, otherwise she could see herself getting lost fast. She looked back. Could she see the cabins or the lake? They were getting deeper and deeper into the forest, and she could no longer see Camp Eureka.

Bugs buzzed in the background, and the trees overhead shaded them from the sun getting higher in the sky. Gracelyn swatted at a mosquito on her arm and reached inside her fanny pack for more bug spray.

Finally, Ms. Mac stopped at the edge of a small stream and waited for the campers to catch up. She hopped up on a fallen tree that formed a natural bridge over the water. "Now, if you look for balance in nature, you'll find it all over the place. **Newton's First Law of Motion** is all about balance. Remember, when the forces acting on an object are balanced, then there isn't any motion!" Ms. Mac shouted. She turned around with her arms out and crossed the stream like a tight-rope walker at the circus. "You'll be using your balance to follow me! Try it, you'll like it!"

A few boys pretended to flail their arms and fall into the stream.

"I wouldn't do that, Campers!" Ms. Spark warned the boys. "I'm sure there are water moccasins in that water!" The boys leapt out of the water and back onto the fallen-tree bridge.

"Oh! And don't mind the spider webs you see in the tree branches," Ms. Mac noted. "Those are hanging in the balance too! So much science in nature. Isn't it amazing?"

"Um, spider webs?" Gracelyn's eyes went wide, and she held her can of bug spray up like mace.

"Don't worry, Gracelyn. I don't think that anything is going to hurt us out here." Halley said, a bit braver than she felt.

After all the campers crossed the stream, they started to climb up to the top of a hill.

"Newton's First Law also says that when things are in motion they tend to stay in motion which is why you are going to keep moving yourself to the top of this geological formation!" Ms. Mac sang out.

Halley and Gracelyn followed along, crunching on pine needles and swatting at bugs until they reached the top of the hill.

"Do you think there is a point to all of this?" Gracelyn said, huffing, a bit out of breath.

"She's a bit of a loony teacher, but I understand what she means. Don't you?" Halley said.

The campers reached a clearing at the top of the hill. In the clearing stood a giant boulder as big as Ms. Dee's Volkswagen Beetle resting on a pedestal of smaller rocks.

"And this, Campers, is where nature can paint a picture worth a thousand words. Welcome to the Famous Balanced Rock of Camp Eureka." Ms. Mac dropped her backpack and nimbly climbed to the top of the boulder. Ms. Spark was the last to join the group, a bit winded from the journey up the hill. She put her hands on the boulder and pulled out a water bottle then rested with her hands on her knees.

"I wonder how that rock got like that," Halley whispered to Nathan.

"Aliens!" Nathan said in a spooky voice.

"This Balanced Rock is a landmark around these parts and an excellent demonstration of balance in nature. This rock has been like this for hundreds of years, and each year I bring campers to the top of this hill to sign their names on a plaque near this boulder.

"But first, let's talk about **Newton's Second Law**

of Motion. Do you think if I were to get a big enough stick and Ms. Spark and I wedged it under that rock, we could force it to move?" Ms. Mac said, smiling.

The campers nervously laughed and a few moved back away from the rock.

"Would it be easier to move this big, balancing rock or a smaller rock?"

"A smaller rock!" the campers sang out in unison.

"Precisely! And that's Newton's Second Law of Motion. To move something big it takes more force than to move something small. In the science world, that is shown by the equation $F=ma$ or force equals mass times acceleration. That's why this rock hasn't moved in hundreds of years because a big enough force has not acted upon it. Neat how that works, right?" Ms. Mac walked around to the plaque filled with hundreds of names.

"Now, I want all of you campers to come over here and add your name on this plaque on the Balanced Rock to mark your first full day here at Camp Eureka before we start our challenge."

Halley cautiously walked around the boulder with the other campers and noticed that the plaque had hundred of names signed by past campers. She looked for Cameron's name and Nathan's name since she knew this wasn't their first time at camp. She took a permanent marker the teen counselors were handing out and signed her name complete with a comet trailing off the "Y" in Halley.

Gracelyn drew her name with a rainbow coming out of it.

"Once you've signed it, please come over here for

your motion challenge." Ms. Mac sang as she walked toward the shade of a few trees.

Halley waited for Gracelyn and already was feeling a little less out of place now that she had signed her name along the other campers that had come before her. They walked over to a challenge station together that had a pile of balloons, string, tape, and straws.

"Now onto my favorite law of motion! **Newton's Third Law** states for every action there is an equal and opposite reaction! This brings us to our first camp challenge and a riddle. The first team to decipher the riddle and complete the challenge will win! Good luck!"

Blast off into the sky
You'll see me moving by
Off to the moon into the stars
This law of motion could get you to Mars.

"Blast off into the sky?" Nathan scratched his head. He picked up the balloons. "Well, surely they are talking about rockets blasting off to Mars."

Halley picked up the challenge materials: balloons, string, tape, and straw… "Hmmm… balloons and rockets." She looked over at Gracelyn who was already smiling. "We know just what to do." Nathan, Gracelyn, and Halley formed a huddle so that the other campers wouldn't hear their plans. They were in it to win it.

"Okay, we're going to be making a balloon rocket. Gracelyn and I have done this one before in my treelab at home," Halley whispered.

"What's a treelab?" Nathan raised his eyebrows.

"Oh, we'll tell you later. For now, let's just say that Gracelyn and I have perfected balloon rockets, and it's a lot of fun!"

"First, take the string and tie it off to one of the trees," Halley instructed Nathan. "Next, Gracelyn, you blow up the balloon while I find the tape to attach the straw on the top. Then I'll thread the string through the straw, and when its time, we'll let the balloon go and it should move along the string all the way to the tree."

"Right-o!" Gracelyn smiled and started blowing up the balloon. Then she stopped and looked at Halley with a slightly red face.

"Houston, we have a problem." Gracelyn said. "This balloon has a bunch of holes in it."

Cameron and the other teen counselors were standing near the Balanced Rock too far to hear if they shouted for help. One of the teen counselors was standing on top of it goofing off.

Halley reached inside her red backpack remembering the balloons she had packed that morning. "Oh, here are a few extra balloons I had in my backpack!" She tossed them to Gracelyn.

"Well, that's nifty! What were you doing with all of those balloons?" Nathan said with a smirk.

Halley smiled at him and shrugged. Good thing Ms. Spark was too far away to hear them joking with each other.

A few other teams had figured out the riddle and were already blowing up their balloons. Halley wondered why their balloon seemed to be the only one that had holes in it.

Halley taped the straw onto the blown up balloon

and threaded the string in the straw. Gracelyn and Nathan ran over and stood by the tree ready to receive the balloon rocket on the other end. "Okay, I'm ready! Are you?" Halley shouted to her teammates.

"Let her rip!" Nathan started a countdown. "10, 9, 8, 7, 6, 5, 4, 3, 2, 1…"

Halley reached down and let go of the end of the balloon.

Ppppfffffttttt! The balloon sailed along the string while it deflated. The air coming from behind pushed it forward.

"It worked, it worked!" Halley and Gracelyn jumped up and down giggling while Nathan clapped.

"Congratulations, Team Comets!" Ms. Mac announced, running up to their balloon rocket. "You have completed the challenged by demonstrating Newton's Third Law of Motion.

Nathan and Gracelyn joined Halley, and they gave each other high fives. "When did you choose our team name?" Halley whispered back at Nathan.

He grinned. "I had to pick a name, and you weren't here to object!"

"What I want to know is, how did our balloon end up with holes in it?" Gracelyn whispered to Halley, still inspecting the balloon cut full of holes.

"Probably just a mistake," Nathan reassured her.

But Halley had a sinking feeling that it was not a mistake. She took the balloon from Gracelyn and turned it over in her hand. The balloon had been sabotaged.

Suddenly, Halley heard someone screaming.

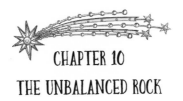

CHAPTER 10

THE UNBALANCED ROCK

CAMERON WAS SCREAMING WHILE THE Balanced Rock started to teeter on its pedestal. The other teen counselors had darted away from the boulder, but Cameron stood frozen in its path. If she didn't move, the Balanced Rock would come right at her.

Halley ran toward Cameron. Why wasn't she getting out of the way? What could have made the huge Balanced Rock move? Halley couldn't move fast enough. Her feet felt stuck in Oobleck, and she could only move in slow motion. Could she get to Cameron in time?

"Stop, Halley!" someone shouted from the crowd.

"Cameron! Move out of the way!" someone else screamed.

"Move!" Halley yelled as she flew through the air,

arms outstretched toward Cameron.

The Balanced Rock barely missed the girls and landed with a thud on a nearby rock wall. The girls were tangled up on the ground, and dust from the rock and their tackle kicked up around them.

Halley looked down at Cameron. She felt like she had tackled a sack of bones. Cameron looked like she wasn't quite sure what hit her.

Gracelyn rushed towards them. "Halley, what were you thinking? You and Cameron could have been crushed!"

Cameron stood, looking stunned. "You saved my life." She stared at the younger camper a foot shorter than her.

"What is the meaning of this?" Ms. Spark snapped as she pushed through the crowd forming around the girls. Her face looked like she was wading through a sea of cockroaches the way she avoided touching anyone's sweatiness. "We will not tolerate this behavior, Miss Harper! Why on earth would you knock her down?"

"She saved her life!" Gracelyn shouted over the crowd of kids talking. "Didn't you see it?"

"Oh, my lands. Cameron, are you okay?" Ms. Mac reached the girls, putting her arms around them. "What happened, dear?"

"All I know is that the Balanced Rock moved, and I just froze." Cameron scratched her head.

"Well, we're going to get to the bottom of this, won't we, Ms. Mac?" Ms. Spark looked over the rim of her glasses. "This is certainly not camp protocol on safety and certainly not behavior befitting of someone attending this camp."

"Let's not jump to conclusions, Beverly." Ms. Mac touched her shaking hands to her forehead. She walked over to the rock to inspect it.

"Ms. Mac, Camp Eureka could close down for this type of incident. We might as well close this session down immediately. Camp Eureka is going to be held accountable for destruction of this landmark," Ms. Spark pointed out.

"Let's discuss this back at camp." Ms. Mac urged the campers to pack up their belongings.

"Close Camp Eureka?" Gracelyn whispered to Halley along the way. "I guess that would mean that we all would be sent home early."

Halley looked back at the Balanced Rock. Well, now she guessed it would be the Unbalanced Rock as it rested on the rock wall. She couldn't believe she had just pushed Cameron out of the way of its path. She walked over to the plaque that she had signed moments before and touched it with her fingers. Would they be the last campers to sign it? Halley felt sad at the thought.

On their hike back to Camp Eureka, Halley walked along with Cameron and Gracelyn in silence. Halley didn't feel much like talking to anyone.

Cameron gave Halley a big hug before they were dismissed from activities for the afternoon. Ms. Mac awarded all of the campers a coupon to visit the General Store.

"I can't wait to try that color-changing Popsicle!" Halley was more excited than she had been since the morning challenge.

"I think I saw some unicorn-colored slime," Gracelyn said, grinning. "Let's go check it out!"

Despite the scary near miss, they were having a lot of fun at camp and spent the afternoon hanging out, licking color-changing Popsicles, and swimming in Lake Archimedes.

That evening, Halley had a nagging feeling that someone had tampered with their balloon rocket. She also found it strange that someone was able to move the Balance Rock without being noticed. But most of all, Halley wondered if Ms. Spark would figure out who was behind the shaving cream avalanche and seek revenge.

That night Halley had more than enough to write in her diary.

Tuesday
Dear Diary,

I got up close and personal with Newton's Laws of Motion today. The first law states: An object at rest stays at rest and an object in motion stays in motion unless acted on by an outside force. Ms. Mac did an amazing magic trick showing us how objects have to overcome friction to move.

She also pointed out how many things in nature are balanced like a tree bridge over a stream, spooky spider webs, and an amazing Balanced Rock (technically now it is the Unbalanced Rock!). Some outside force caused the Balanced Rock to fall, but gravity made it roll downhill and almost over Cameron and me! Ouch! Newton's Second law would tell us that a large force would have to move a rock that is that heavy. I hope Ms. Mac gets to the bottom of it!

The best part of the day was learning about the third law of motion: for every action there is an equal but opposite reaction. We won the challenge by making a balloon rocket. Blast off!

Ms. Mac announced at dinner tonight that Camp Eureka would not be closing this session. I'm glad, I really like it here. I guess I should just enjoy it as much as I can while I'm here.

Tata for now! I hope I get up on time tomorrow!

PS. The color-changing Popsicle is amazing.

CHAPTER 11

BRAINS ARE IN MOTION

HALLEY AND GRACELYN DECIDED THEY did not want to be late on the second day of camp. Gracelyn set her rainbow alarm clock she had brought from home, and Halley set her watch that she wore to bed. When they got to Pie Are Square dining hall before the other campers, the only thing ready to eat were blueberry muffins, so they decided to eat outside on some picnic tables by Lake Archimedes.

The morning was still very quiet and pleasantly cool. A misty fog hovered right over the lake.

"Hey, Gracelyn." Halley peeled back more of her blueberry muffin cupcake holder. "Do you think that I'm a little weird?" She took too big a bite of muffin and had a hard time swallowing the muffin and the words.

"Weird in what way?" Gracelyn inspected her friend. "Don't we all have our little quirks?" She reached inside her fanny pack and squirted some hand sanitizer over her sticky, blueberry-covered hands.

"I don't know. Sometimes I just don't feel like I fit in. Especially after my mom called me a square peg in a round hole." Halley looked off in the distance beyond the lake.

Gracelyn came around the picnic table to sit on the same side as Halley. She put her arm around her. "You're my best friend, Halley, and there is no one I'd rather feel a little out of place with than you."

Halley looked over at her friend and smiled and then spotted something moving in the woods in the distance. A young deer bent down to eat grass on the other side of the lake. Its legs looked a little too long for its body, and its ears looked too big for its head. Then, as if it knew it was being watched, it lifted its head and locked eyes with the girls across the lake.

"I really like it here," Halley whispered.

"Yeah, me too," Gracelyn whispered back. Suddenly, the deer darted back into the woods just as the other campers started piling out of Pie Are Square and followed Ms. Mac as she strolled to the edge of the lake with Ms. Spark.

Halley was sure no one noticed the deer. She was glad it was going to be a special moment between friends.

"Good morning, Science Campers!" Ms. Mac chirped. When the campers didn't listen, she blew a whistle hanging around her neck to get their attention. "Let's not beat around the bush. The events of yesterday were disturbing, but we must not let it get us down. We must remember that science and discovery must go on!"

Halley looked over at the teen counselors and Cameron, who didn't seem disturbed. Ms. Mac and Ms. Spark must have given them a pep talk before today's challenge. Halley hoped she gave them a safety talk too.

"Why can't these challenges be inside one of the cool air-conditioned buildings?" Gracelyn whispered as they followed Ms. Mac down a trail away from the campsite.

Halley agreed as she wiped the back of her sweaty neck. It wasn't even the afternoon, and the humidity was making it hard to be comfortable outside. "You know what they say about Texas weather. If you don't like it, wait a day and it will change."

"Yeah, from hot to hotter," Gracelyn joked.

Nathan caught up to the girls when Ms. Mac finally stopped the campers. The area was at least as big as a football field and crisscrossed with wooden fences between the trees. And when they turned the corner, they saw a wooden entrance with a sign that said, "The Maze of Science!"

"What is a maze of science?" Halley swatted away a mosquito but was too late. It bit her before she squished it on her hand. Dang mosquitoes. She had forgotten to put mosquito repellent on and was regretting it. The bite stung, and it began to rise up into an ugly pink bump.

Nathan wiped beads of sweat from his forehead, and Gracelyn picked at her fingernail polish that was mostly gone.

"Science can be a bit of a puzzle at times," Ms. Mac told the campers. "We think we know the answers, and sometimes it just doesn't work out that way." Ms. Mac rubbed a bit of sweat forming over her missing brow. "You are about to enter the one and only Camp Eureka Maze of Science. Instead of me teaching you today, perhaps you can find out the answers to the puzzle for yourself within the maze! There are items to collect along the way and build into the Laws of Motion. There are two rules I need you to remember. Rule number one is to wear the helmets that you will find inside the maze for your safety. The second rule is you must stick with your team. The first team to make it through to the finish line by solving the riddle will win today's challenge!"

Halley looked at Nathan and Gracelyn who had perked up when they heard maze. They all nodded, accepting the challenge. Halley gulped, imagining what would happen to the team that got stuck inside the maze.

"On your mark, get set, go!" Ms. Mac blew her whistle.

The campers jumped and stampeded over each other to get into the maze first.

"Oh my goodness, I love mazes!" Gracelyn squealed as she ran into the maze.

Halley looked at the wooden fenced walls three times as tall as her and got a sinking feeling of being trapped. She started popping her fingers nervously before catching herself. Dad said it was such a bad habit. She wiped her sweaty hands on her shorts.

"This is going to be awesome, Halley!" Nathan looked at Halley, who had fallen behind them. "But we've got to be quicker! Look, a few campers have already reached the first station!" Nathan ran ahead of them, looking at the first clue.

Ms. Mac didn't disappoint when the first station was a helmet. The sign above the table holding the helmets read:

Attempt Newton's Law
Better be safe than sorry
Brains are in motion

Halley smirked at the poetry, and she thought back to the haiku she liked to write in her treelab. Nice touch, Ms. Mac.

The kids picked up the helmets and kept running through the maze, which was harder than they expected it to be. They would get to one end and have to turn around and find a different way out. Some of the walls weren't fully covered with vines so they could see the other campers running in opposite directions giggling.

"I feel like mice looking for cheese!" Gracelyn said, frustrated when they reached a dead end and had to turn around again.

Halley sucked her front teeth in like a mouse. Maybe if she joked around with Gracelyn she would stop feeling claustrophobic, like the walls were going to trap them.

"Stop goofing around, Halley! This is serious." Nathan pulled on her arm. "We've got to get out of the maze and win this challenge!"

Halley ran to keep up with Nathan and Gracelyn, but a low buzzing noise started ringing in her ears. Out of the corner of her eye, between the wooden slats she saw Ms. Spark in the maze. What was she doing in here? Maybe she was going to help any campers that get stuck in the maze. Maybe she would help Halley if she started to faint from claustrophobia.

Ms. Spark was quickly walking, holding her clipboard. Halley peered through the slats to get a better look at what she was doing and wondered where the teen counselors were.

Gracelyn led them through the maze to the next clue where five skateboards were propped up against the wall. Each skateboard had a team name written on them.

"We have two teams ahead of us!" Gracelyn panted.

Nathan picked up the one that had "Team Comet" written on it and read the next clue:

Friction stops motion
A wheel and axle can help
Get on, sit down, win!

"Awesome skateboard!" Nathan put a foot on the board, ready to push off.

"No, wait!" Halley insisted. "We need to stay together. Just pick it up, and let's run ahead." She was scared she'd get lost, but didn't want Nathan and Gracelyn to know that.

"Come on, y'all, I see the next clue!" Gracelyn peered around the corner of the maze.

They saw something red. The third clue. They ran up to it, and saw that it was a fire extinguisher.

"Where are the other teams that were ahead of us?" Nathan said, smirking.

"They must have gotten lost in the maze!" Gracelyn beamed. Then she read the next clue:

Remove pin and squeeze
It's filled with pressure and force!
Makes a great rocket!

"What in the world are we going to do with a fire extinguisher?" Halley looked down with her nose scrunched up. "Are we putting out forest fires riding along on a skateboard?"

"No, silly. Remember this is all about Newton's Laws," Gracelyn said.

Halley looked at Gracelyn, impressed. She was really getting into this challenge. Halley was glad that Gracelyn was so good at mazes, because all Halley wanted to do was climb over the walls and be done with the challenge.

"Hey, here's the exit!" Gracelyn said.

Halley stepped out from the maze onto a long straight road with trees on either side. She breathed a deep sigh, looking up at the sun. "I hate mazes," she whispered to Gracelyn, as she recognized the road as the entrance to camp.

"Pull yourself together, Halley. We need you to help us figure out what to do with this stuff." Gracelyn nudged Halley. They stepped up to the road and noticed racing lines were painted on the asphalt.

"Okay." Halley blew out some air to compose herself. "Let's see what we've got here. A helmet, a fire extinguisher, and a skateboard." A light bulb went off in her head. "I got it! Gracelyn, here, you put on this helmet!"

"Why me?" Gracelyn protested. "I got you out of the maze, remember? No, it should be your turn!"

"Remember, the second law of motion says that a smaller mass will go faster. So you're in luck. You are going to be the pilot of our skateboard rocket!

"Skateboard what?!" Gracelyn strapped the helmet on her head.

"You've got to get on backwards and sit down. Remember the second riddle? Get on, sit down, win?" Halley hurried to help Gracelyn to sit down. "We don't have much time now!"

"Aw! No fair. I wanted to ride the rocket!" Nathan shouted.

A few of the kids were catching on and setting up to race them. Halley saw Ms. Mac about fifty yards away from them, smiling with her hands on her hips at a tape saying, "Finish Line."

Ms. Spark stood next to her holding a squirt bottle and her clipboard. She shaded her eyes from the sun and started tapping her foot annoyed.

"Hold this tight, Gracelyn." Halley handed her the fire extinguisher. "Nathan, you pull the pin and, Gracelyn, press down on this handle and hang on."

"This is going to be so stinking cool!" Nathan sang.

Gracelyn hugged the fire extinguisher tighter, looking at Halley as if she was crazy.

"Remember, don't lean left or right. Just sit still and press down. You'll go in a straight line to reach the finish line and win!"

Other campers were starting to pile out of the maze, but Gracelyn was already sitting down preparing to blast off.

"This is going to be amazing!" Halley shouted to Gracelyn.

Gracelyn gave her a big thumbs-up and pushed the lever down. White clouds spewed from the fire extinguisher. The force from the fire extinguisher slowly moved Gracelyn backwards on the skateboard. Then she picked up speed. The white clouds made it hard to see Gracelyn, but she was the first team racing towards the finish line.

Halley wanted to support her friend to the finish line so she started running beside her. Gracelyn had a huge smile, but her nose was all crinkled up trying to push down hard on the fire extinguisher and not lose her balance. Ms. Mac was at the finish line jumping up and down in excitement.

Suddenly, Gracelyn veered off the straight path and headed full steam toward a line of trees beside the road. She screamed, and the skateboard started going haywire. Gracelyn was still pressing down on the fire extinguisher when one of the skateboard wheels fell off. The skateboard rocket took a sharp turn, and Gracelyn's body went in the opposite direction as it flung her off. She reached her hands out to keep from running into a tree.

The fire extinguisher clanked on the road and spun to a stop.

"Gracelyn!" Halley ran toward her best friend who lay crumpled on the ground.

CHAPTER 12
LEFTY LOOSEY

"GRACELYN! OH NO!" HALLEY RAN toward her best friend. "Are you okay? What happened?" She looked at Gracelyn and then looked around for help.

Ms. Mac ran towards them, the whistle dangling around her neck swinging back and forth like a pendulum.

Ms. Spark walked slowly up to them, inspecting the situation and scratching furiously on her clipboard. A few campers exiting the maze ran up to see what had happened.

Gracelyn sat on her knees, holding her wrist with tears squirting out of her face as she looked up at Halley.

A lump rose in Halley's throat. "Gracelyn, I'm so sorry. I should have been on the skateboard rocket!" She couldn't believe all the disasters. And this time, it was her best friend on the receiving end of it.

Nathan grabbed the skateboard, turning it over in his hand, inspecting it. "The axle nuts on the wheels are not the only things that are loose. So are the truck mounting bolts."

Halley was impressed by how much Nathan knew about skateboards. She was certain all of the nuts and bolts should not have been loose on a skateboard meant as a human rocket.

"My arm is broken!" Gracelyn winced. Her face was white, and she held her wrist close to her body.

"Gracelyn, dear, what happened? You were blasting off on that amazing rocket and then landed like a sack of potatoes!" Ms. Mac looked down at Gracelyn and back up at Halley. "Well don't fret. We'll get you to the medic and then call your parents." Ms. Mac helped Gracelyn up and tried to keep away the curious onlookers.

"I'm coming with you," Halley said before Ms. Mac could object. Halley had never had a broken bone before, but she could see how much pain Gracelyn was in and didn't want her to be scared.

"Well, alright dear." Ms. Mac looked concerned. "Gracelyn, is that alright?"

"Yes, please just help me." Tears ran down Gracelyn's face.

"Something is wrong here." Nathan said under his breath and frowned. "This other wheel is loose."

"What do you mean?" Halley tried to pry her attention off her hurt friend to listen to Nathan. She gave it a spin and the screw popped out, the second wheel fell to the ground. "Lefty loosey, righty tighty,"

Halley said, thinking aloud.

"What?" Nathan held the skateboard in his hand.

"Lefty loosey, righty tighty." Halley examined the wheel. "Someone tampered with the skateboard and unscrewed the wheels so it wouldn't work properly." For the first time since she came to camp, Halley was scared someone really wanted them to leave.

"This does look weird, Halley," Nathan said, worried. "But who would want to win the race so badly that they would sabotage the skateboard?"

"I don't know." Halley grumbled as she left Nathan to catch up with Ms. Mac and Gracelyn walking to the medic. When Halley caught up to them, she got a sinking feeling that maybe this was meant for her instead.

Ms. Mac looked genuinely worried for Gracelyn, who had started sobbing.

Tears welled up in Halley's eyes, seeing her friend in pain. It was Gracelyn who wanted her to come to sleep-away camp with her. It was Gracelyn that was so excited for the adventure they would have. So what if Halley was starting to feel like less of a square peg here at camp? Maybe this should be the final session of Camp Eureka for good before anyone else got hurt.

CHAPTER 13

SCIENCE GIRL EXTRAORDINAIRE

WHEN THEY REACHED THE MEDIC, Ms. Mac turned and looked at Halley. "Gracelyn may be in the medic for a while, and I'm going to give her mother a call to let her know what happened. I'm sure you are shaken up, dear. Can you go back to your cabin and rest? We'll let you know what happens."

Halley nodded and gave Gracelyn a little smile before she turned to plod back to Cabin Curie. She just didn't think she could sit alone in her cabin and wait or even go get lunch with the rest of the campers. She was looking down, kicking a rock when she bumped into Nathan.

"Hey, how's Gracelyn?" Nathan asked.

"Oh, hey, Nathan." Halley's thoughts were interrupted. "Where is that skateboard? I wanted to look at it again."

"Oh, Ms. Spark took it and said she needed it for the investigation. Don't worry, they'll get to the bottom of this." But he didn't look so convinced.

"At this rate, there are too many disasters to figure out." Halley stared across the campground. "I just want to make this all better, especially for Gracelyn."

Nathan nodded in agreement.

"Hey, what's going on over there?" Halley perked up, noticing colorful balloons pinned onto targets in the distance.

"An archery course." Nathan smiled. "A few of the teen counselors set it up and said we were free to play after lunch." It was the first time he looked cheery since the accident.

"Come on. Let's go check it out." Halley ran towards the archery course. When they got there, it looked like the object of the game was to pop the balloons by hitting a bull's-eye.

"Kind of reminds me of water balloons." Nathan elbowed Halley.

It seemed like such a long time ago since Nathan hit Halley in the back with a water balloon. But now she secretly wanted to hit a bull's-eye before Nathan did.

They each grabbed a bow and some arrows. Nathan lined up next to Halley with his back to her. Cameron was there too and had already shot several bull's-eyes. She smiled and waved to them.

Halley held the bow in one hand and placed the arrow gently on the arrow rest. She could see the balloon waving in the breeze. The clouds were building, and it was threatening to rain. It was hard for her not to think about Gracelyn holding her broken arm and the Balance Rock tipping over, almost crushing Cameron. She pulled back the arrow, took a deep breath, and let go.

The arrow soared high over the target. It wasn't even close to the balloon.

"Oh, man," Halley said under her breath, hoping Nathan hadn't seen.

"You know," Nathan said, loading his arrow. His back was turned so Halley couldn't really see his face. "I'm so impressed by you."

"Did you not see? I missed!" Halley said, defending her last miss.

"No, really, Halley. You really impress me by how well you fit in here and how brave you are. You are like a science girl extraordinaire. Back at home, I feel so out of place. I really don't want to go back to school this fall. My teachers don't get me. My parents don't get me, and Camp Eureka is really the only place I can come and be myself. I don't know what I'd do if I couldn't come back to Camp Eureka next summer."

"You like it here that much?" Halley didn't tell Nathan how much she loved school and her teachers but nodded in agreement. Would Mom call him a square peg in a round hole too?

"Yeah, and how else would I have met you?" Nathan pulled back and let the arrow go. It landed close to the bull's-eye but didn't pop the balloon.

Halley felt her cheeks getting red.

"You're brave enough to push someone out of the way of getting crushed and at the same time pulling an epic prank on ol' Spark." Nathan turned his head towards her, his eyes twinkling. "Promise we'll write each other if we don't come back next summer? We could write all about our latest science experiments and inventions at home."

"Um sure, Nate." All the compliments embarrassed Halley a little. She hadn't thought about the next time she would see Nathan, especially if Camp Eureka closed. She also hadn't considered that maybe she wasn't the only one that felt a little out of place in the real world.

Halley felt lucky to have met a boy like Nathan at camp. Her head swirled with science as she got another arrow and loaded it. She thought about Ms. Mac and Newton's cradle. She thought about Dad and Ben. She thought of all the things she was learning at camp that she was going to write in her diary to send to *Empower With Science* magazine. She pulled the arrow back, took a deep breath, focused on the red balloon waving in the breeze, and let go.

POP!

As if on cue, it started to rain.

"Come on, let's go check on Gracelyn," Halley said. They started running toward the buildings for cover.

They ducked into Energy Hall on their way to the medic building to avoid getting drenched. They walked quietly by Ms. Mac's office. Her door was slightly closed, but Halley could hear voices from inside.

"Yep, I'm afraid so," Ms. Mac sighed. "With all of these accidents and now we don't have the funds to keep it open? We'll be lucky if we can close out the last day tomorrow. We'll have to tell the campers first and then their parents that this will be the last Camp Eureka before it's shut down indefinitely."

CHAPTER 14
FRICTION STOPS MOTION

D ID I JUST HEAR HER say that they are going to shut down camp?" Halley couldn't believe it.

"That's what it sounded like to me." Nathan nodded.

She was sure it was because Gracelyn had broken her arm. But what did Ms. Mac mean about not enough money to keep it open? As they walked down the hall, Halley thought about Mom and how she had banned messy science experiments at her house. If Camp Eureka closed, would Halley ever do science again?

They reached the medic's door and knocked. No one answered. "Gracelyn must have gone back to the cabin," Halley said.

"What if we hold a fundraiser to keep Camp Eureka open?" Nathan suggested as they walked back to

Cabin Curie.

"How could us kids ever raise enough money to keep this huge camp open?" Halley asked. "And what about all the accidents?"

"What if they weren't accidents?" Nathan frowned as they reached the cabin.

"I don't know, Nate." Halley pushed her way through the door.

Gracelyn was sitting on the lower bunk bed looking at an amazing rainbow cast on her arm.

"Gracelyn!" Halley ran to hug her best friend. "Are you okay? We were so worried about you! Are you going to have to go home now?"

"No, Mom said as long as I'm okay then I can stay another day." Gracelyn ran her fingers over the brightly-colored cast. "I broke my wrist, so I'll need to stay in this cast for most of the summer."

"Well, guess what we heard on the way here?" Halley plopped down on the floor. "We overheard Ms. Mac say that Camp Eureka would be closing. We've got to do something to keep it open."

"I know! Even though I broke my arm, this place keeps getting cooler and cooler." Gracelyn reached for some astronaut ice cream that she got from the medic and took a big bite.

"Hey, where's my ice cream?" Halley questioned.

"Sorry, just for kids who break bones." Gracelyn smirked. "Hey, you need to sign my cast!" Gracelyn reached for a marker. "And check out how Ms. Mac signed it!"

Halley got up and touched Ms. Mac's signature. It read, "Friction stops motion – so do arms. Get well soon, Love Ms. Mac."

"She's pretty cool." Halley sighed. "So let's enjoy camp while it lasts and end it with a bang!"

That night Halley wrote:

Wednesday
Dear Diary,

Tomorrow may be the last full day of Camp Eureka unless we figure out a way to keep it going. There have been a lot of scary accidents here. Gracelyn even broke her arm, but she did get a pretty awesome rainbow cast though!

I'll miss the campers if this really is the end. Tomorrow is the camp-wide Color War Challenge. It will be red vs. blue. I hope that we are on the same team as Cameron.

Today we learned about how friction stops motion (and apparently so does Gracelyn's arm – ouch!) To overcome friction, you can use a wheel and axle like in a skateboard (as long as it's screwed on tight!)

Lefty Loosey, Righty Tighty,
Halley

P.S. I'm going to miss a lot of campers when I get home. I hope they'll write me over the summer. We can even be pen pals!

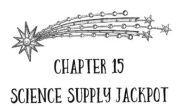

CHAPTER 15
SCIENCE SUPPLY JACKPOT

HALLEY AND GRACELYN WOKE UP excited to compete in the camp Color Wars. They found out they were going to be on the red team when they were given silly headbands, red t-shirts, and long, silly red socks to wear. The teen counselors passing out the gear reminded them to wear their swimsuits under their clothes for the day.

Halley was excited that she was on her favorite-color team. The girls painted their faces with red stripes with lipstick that Gracelyn had brought from home.

Pie Are Square was buzzing with excitement during breakfast. Everyone was dressed in their team colors. Nathan joined them wearing a red headband.

"What are the games going to be?" Halley asked around a mouthful of waffles.

"I think it's going to be some type of bowling

game," Nathan said. "Last year we had games that cooled us off since it was so hot outside."

"Tomorrow is the fun day, though, because we get to recreate our favorite science experiment to show our parents. It's the camp's way of convincing them to bring us back next year." Nathan's voice trailed off.

"But there's not going to be a next year." Gracelyn frowned.

"We'll figure something out, y'all. Let's just make the most of today and win one for Team Red!" Halley said.

Her stomach was full of powdered sugar, syrup, and waffles when they walked outside after breakfast, and she almost wished she hadn't had so much to eat. It was going to be another hot day. Halley regretted not putting on some sunscreen as she pulled her hair back into a ponytail.

"Whew, it's going to be scorcher." Gracelyn squirted water in her mouth from her bottle.

"Good morning, Campers!" Ms. Mac sang out. If Ms. Mac was a morning person, Ms. Spark definitely was not. She stood next to Ms. Mac, scowling. "Now that you are all here, Ms. Spark and I have an announcement to make. Drastic times call for drastic measures…"

"Yes, thank you, Ms. Mac, I'll take it from here," Ms. Spark interrupted.

Halley and Gracelyn looked at each other, surprised.

"After completing a thorough safety review of this camp, a decision has been made to close Camp Eureka forever. It was a difficult decision, but it is for the best."

Ms. Spark peered over the top of her glasses.

The colorful red and blue campers gasped. "Why?" a few boys yelled out.

"Thank you, Ms. Spark for stealing my thunder," Ms. Mac snapped. "We'll be sending out a camp letter with you tomorrow to take home to your parents. It has been my honor and privilege to have led this camp for ten years." She wiped a tear out of the corner of her eye and took off her visor.

"Thank you, Ms. Mac, for the sentiment, but let's get going so we can finish up." Ms. Spark interrupted again, tapping her foot and pointing to her watch.

"Right. Okay, teen counselors, take it away!" Ms. Mac said, pulling herself together and firmly placing her visor back on her head. "Campers, don't forget to use your heads, and may the best color win!"

The teen counselors were dressed up in their team colors and led the campers to a giant tarp laid over the campgrounds. They directed the campers to split up, red team on the left of the tarp and blue team on the right. At the end of the tarp were giant blow-up bowling pins.

"The object of the game is to be the first team to knock down the most bowling pins on this giant water slide!" a counselor shouted.

"Thank goodness for a water activity." Halley crossed her arms and squinted in the sunlight.

"A water slide! That sounds amazing!" Gracelyn cheered. "But wait, I don't think I can get my cast wet, right?"

"Oh, that's no problem," Halley reassured Grace-lyn. "My cousin had a cast and just wrapped it in plastic when they went to the splash pad last summer. I'll just run back to Pie Are Square to get some plastic wrap and something to tie it with."

"I don't want you to miss all the fun." Gracelyn sighed.

"I'll be back in a flash." Halley smiled and hugged her friend.

"Okay, well, hurry back. We'll need our whole team together to win," Nathan warned.

Halley raced off towards Pie Are Square. She was secretly glad to get back into the air conditioning, if only for a minute. She was already feeling a bit light-headed from the heat.

She pushed open the door. The dining hall had already been cleaned and cleared from breakfast. It was empty and the lights were out. It seemed like the whole camp was out enjoying the Color War. She went into the kitchen and found the pantry easily. Surely something was in here. She opened the door and marveled at everything the pantry stocked.

"Wow, I never knew how amazing a science camp pantry would be." She stepped inside and turned on the lights. She ran her fingers over huge bags of cornstarch, glue, vinegar, baking soda, and vegetable oil. There were supply bins labeled with all sorts of experiments. "Lava Lamps" and "S'mores" and "Oobleck." Halley stood staring at all the supplies with her mouth open. She'd hit the science supply jackpot. There, right next to the air conditioning control box, was a tube of plastic wrap. "Perfect! Now I've got to get back to the Color Wars quick!"

She glanced at the "Oobleck" supply bin, and it

reminded her of home. Suddenly, she heard the pantry door starting to shut behind her.

"Wait, no!" Halley reached for the door, but it slammed shut. She tried the doorknob, but it was locked from the outside. She was locked in the pantry alone!

"Okay, not funny. Nathan, are you pulling a prank on me? You know I don't like being in small spaces." Halley started breathing a little faster.

She heard another voice outside the pantry. It was Ms. Spark.

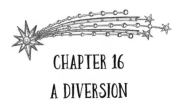

CHAPTER 16
A DIVERSION

HALLEY PUT HER EAR UP to the door to hear it better. She got a bad case of déjà vu. Who was Ms. Spark talking to anyways?

"A science camp for kids is such a joke," Ms. Spark seethed. "Think of all the scientific discoveries that the funds could have been used for instead. Well, I took care of that."

A pause. Was Ms. Spark on the phone with someone?

"Oh, you know Mac was never one to be very good with money. She'll never know I've been draining the camp of funds this summer. She won't find out that the safety review of the camp was really a way to close it for good. Trust me; I was trying to shut the camp down by scaring the kids off. I never meant to hurt anyone. Really. But the best part is Mac will never trace it back to me. She thinks that these kids are being too competitive. She said they are having some good, fun camp rivalry. Well, this is the last year. I'm putting a stop to science camp nonsense once and for all. Especially once the parents find out about all the accidents. Oh, and don't forget this. No one, I mean no one, pulls a prank on Spark and gets away with it."

Halley couldn't believe what she was hearing. It was Ms. Spark this whole time. She was behind all of the accidents because she was trying to shut the camp down. And now she was stealing money from camp. She would be so mad if she knew that Halley had heard all of that.

What if Ms. Spark caught her eavesdropping in the pantry? How was she going to get out of here? Halley started popping her fingers nervously. "Okay, think, Halley, think." Surely Gracelyn and Nathan were going to get worried and come looking for her. But the last thing she wanted was for them to run into Ms. Spark. Think, Halley, think. She was locked in a pantry full of science stuff. Surely she could figure out how to create some type of diversion.

What if Ms. Spark was trying to sabotage the Color Wars too? Was someone else going to get hurt before she could warn them? Would someone get hurt if she wasn't there to save them? She had to get out of there and tell someone.

The camp's air conditioning control panel was right next to the plastic wrap! She remembered how hot it was outside, and without air conditioning, it would be unbearable in the buildings too. All she needed to do was find the off switch on the panel, and within a few minutes, Pie Are Square was going to be so hot Ms. Spark would want to leave. She reached for the control box, found the switch, and flipped it off.

The air conditioning shuttered to a stop. "Hang on, it feels like the AC kicked off." Ms. Spark muttered.

Halley saw a shadow move underneath the door. Then silence. She could be locked in this pantry for a while before anyone found her. She plopped down on a bag of cornstarch and powder flew in the air, filling the pantry. Her nose started itching. She heard someone turn the doorknob, and the lock clicked.

Aaachoo! Halley tried to stifle her sneeze. This was it. She was going to be found out.

But the shadow moved, and Halley heard footsteps walking away from the pantry. She tried to stifle another sneeze when she realized she wasn't locked in anymore! She waited a few minutes, stood, dusted the cornstarch off her shorts, and slowly opened the pantry door.

She poked her head out of the pantry and realized how hot it was already getting in Pie Are Square with no air conditioning. Then she grabbed the plastic wrap, made a run for the door, and darted back out to the Color Wars. By now, Nathan and Gracelyn would be worried about her.

By the time she arrived back at the giant water slide, Ms. Mac and Ms. Spark were standing next to each other.

"Hello, Miss Harper, where have you been?" Ms. Spark questioned.

"Uh, I had to go to the bathroom," Halley managed to say before she ran and dove onto the water slide. She wasn't about to stick around and get asked questions.

It was funny how all the campers were laughing and having a great time. They had no idea what was really happening to Camp Eureka. Halley had a hard time pretending to enjoy the rest of the Color War games. There was never a good time to tell Gracelyn or Nathan what she overheard. Would they even believe her that Ms. Spark was sabotaging Camp Eureka?

CHAPTER 17

CAMPFIRE CONFESSION

THE CAMPFIRE CRACKLED, AND THE campers' faces glowed while they were sitting in little huddles making s'mores. But s'mores couldn't cheer Halley up. She was so upset about everything she had learned about Ms. Spark after being locked in the pantry. And to top that, the blue team ended up winning the Color War, leaving Halley's red team down in the dumps.

S'mores were a great way to unite the campers and help them enjoy their last night, but rumors were flying everywhere about why Camp Eureka was closing. Some campers were telling ghost stories about how the camp must be haunted with ghosts of old scientists. Others were whispering that aliens had taken over Ms. Mac's body.

Gracelyn plopped down next to Halley and poked

a toasted marshmallow in her mouth. "Hey Halley, why were you so down in the dumps during the Color Wars? Weren't you having fun?"

Halley knew she was the only camper who knew the truth. In fact, even Ms. Mac didn't know the truth. She decided she finally had to tell her friends what she heard in the pantry that afternoon.

"You will never believe what I heard when I ran back to Pie Are Square." Halley whispered. "I over-heard Ms. Spark say that she is responsible for closing down the camp." Halley still didn't believe it when she said it.

"What do you mean?" Gracelyn said. "It's not an alien from outer space?"

"No, I'm serious. I actually heard her say that she's trying to tank camp." Halley insisted.

"How are you ever going to prove that?" Nathan muttered, picking at a stick then tossing it into the fire. "Besides, why would Ms. Spark want camp to end? It's her summer job, isn't it?"

"I know it doesn't make any sense. I heard her say that a kids' science camp was not as important as other scientific discoveries and that spending money on this camp is a waste." Halley poked her marshmallow with a skewer and jabbed it towards the fire.

"Wait, I thought you and Gracelyn would be hap-py this camp is over." Nathan tilted his head. "You are the ones having to put up with being the only girl campers here. And look at poor Gracelyn who broke her arm during a challenge." Nathan kept turning his marshmallow on a slow roast.

"Nah, I actually like it here." Halley carefully removed her marshmallow and sandwiched it between a chocolate and graham crackers. "Besides, I like having a place to just do science and be a kid without worrying what kind of mess I'm going to make or if my little brother is going to screw up an experiment. And hey, you're not so bad either." Halley shoved Nathan with her elbow, causing his marshmallow to catch on fire.

"Hey!" Nathan blew out his crispy marshmallow. "Oh well, that's okay. I like them charred a bit!"

"Hey, guys!" A familiar voice said. Halley couldn't see her face until she came closer to the campfire.

"Hey, Cameron!" Halley beamed. "Want to join us for a s'more?"

"I love s'mores. Thanks!" Cameron settled in with them around the fire. "Are y'all sad this is the last camp?"

"Yeah, we were just talking about that." Halley looked toward Gracelyn and Nathan with a don't-say-anything look in her eyes.

"Well, have you heard the rumor going around?" Cameron leaned in closer and looked around.

"Which one? That alien one or the ghost one?" Gracelyn smirked.

"No, really. I overheard my parents talking to Ms. Mac before we left for camp. I almost didn't go to this session because they thought camp was getting too expensive. Ms. Mac was begging that they send me because camp had a greater purpose and would help me as an adult. She said camp needed kids like me to attend. Whatever she said, it convinced my parents."

Halley thought back to the reason she was at camp. It wasn't as important as being summoned by

Ms. Mac. She was only here because this is where she could get out of Mom's hair for a little while. Halley's stomach felt tight and green with jealousy. Why did Mom have to call her weird? She just wanted to be someone special at home and at camp.

"But do you ever wonder about Ms. Mac and Ms. Spark, and why this camp started in the first place?" Cameron interrupted Halley's thought. "They were the original founders, you know."

The campfire spit a few sparks their way and a log shifted in the fire. It was almost as if the fire was getting itself comfortable for a story.

"I heard that Mac and Spark were friends and chemistry lab partners in school." Cameron leaned in closer. "They did a lot of science experiments together and vowed to open this science camp when they grew up. They were awarded a government grant to help teach future scientists and engineers. But while they were planning one of the camp sessions, a lab accident happened. Spark managed to escape, but Mac was burned badly and that is how she lost her eyebrow. Spark felt so bad that she ended up helping Mac teach the camp over the summer when they weren't teaching science during the school year."

"What happened in the accident?" Halley had forgotten about the half-eaten s'more in her hand. She was baffled by what she was hearing.

"I'm not sure. I think it was a nasty fire. But Mac was so passionate about this science camp and how it could help kids change the world that she kept pouring her heart and soul into the camp. Spark, on the other hand, seems like she's grown a bit tired of the kid antics, perhaps even growing bitter. Can't you tell?"

"Look, maybe you should just go talk to Ms. Mac about what you heard, Halley." Gracelyn whispered so Cameron couldn't hear. "Surely she has an answer to it. I'm starting to like this camp too. I never thought I'd like science so much, but I do love it! I want to come back here next year with you!"

Halley's stomach felt like she had one too many s'mores.

"What are you doing for your last-day camp project?" Cameron opened another package of graham crackers.

"I think we need more s'mores to figure it out!" Nathan gulped down another burnt marshmallow.

Halley forced a smile. How could she think about their last-day project after all she found out today? What was she going to say to Ms. Mac, and would she even believe her?

Thursday
Dear Diary,

I don't want this to be my last diary entry on the last night of camp. But I'll make it short. I think I'm allergic to cornstarch. It makes me sneeze! But wow, I could make a load of Oobleck with all that cornstarch in the pantry!

Love,
Halley

PS. We're going to figure out a way to keep Camp Eureka open. I just love this place!

CHAPTER 18

MS. MAC'S HANGOUT

O N THE LAST DAY OF camp, Halley trudged into Energy Hall with her team. They decided to skip breakfast to catch Ms. Mac in her office. They walked by the Newton's cradle she saw the first day of camp. She wasn't even in the mood to swing one of the end balls. When she reached Ms. Mac's office, Halley could see Ms. Mac moving around behind the frosted glass. She hoped Ms. Spark wasn't in there too. A lump formed in her throat that she couldn't swallow down.

She looked back, and Gracelyn and Nathan sat down cross-legged on the floor. Nathan was biting his fingernails, and Gracelyn's face must have mirrored Halley's because she looked a bit scared too. This must be what it felt like to go to the principal's office.

She softly knocked on the door and gulped again.

Ms. Mac opened her door and looked a bit surprised. "Halley? Well, good morning. Can I help you?"

"I needed to talk to you about something in private." Halley peered in the office to check that Ms. Spark wasn't there.

"Well of course, come on in." Ms. Mac stepped aside and led her into her office, closing the door behind her. Ms. Mac sat on her desk and crossed her arms, motioning for Halley to make herself comfortable. "Here, sit down here, my dear."

Ms. Mac's office smelled like peppermint and coffee. It reminded Halley of Christmas. There was a poster of Albert Einstein with his tongue sticking out hung on the wall. It was captioned: "I have no special talent. I'm just passionately curious." Next to that poster hung another colorful poster with a child looking at a rainbow, and it said, "Every possibility exists in a child's mind." Halley already felt a little at ease.

"Did you enjoy camp, Halley?" Ms. Mac surveyed Halley's face. "I've been very impressed by you and your team. You have a special talent."

"Well, um, yes." Halley said, nervously popping a knuckle then shaking out her hand. "I guess that is what I want to talk to you about. I overheard someone talking about camp, and I needed to tell you about it."

"Oh, I see." Ms. Mac looked down and shifted her weight."I'm sure the rumor mill is running rampant. Tell me, Halley, what did you hear on the grapevine?"

"Well, you see…" Halley stuttered, looking for the right words then just blurted out, "I was in the pantry looking for plastic wrap, and I got locked in."

Ms. Mac's eyes got wider as she listened.

"I was really scared because I'm claustrophobic and was trying to get out when I overheard Ms. Spark talking to someone about ending the camp and how much she didn't like camp. How much the funds were being wasted on us kids." Halley felt a big weight lift off her chest, but after her rant there was an awkward silence. She started popping her knuckles again when Ms. Mac didn't say anything.

Did she just give Ms. Mac too much information? Would she get in trouble for being in the pantry and trying to take something?

"Oh, Ms. Spark? Let me tell you about old Spark, Halley. She is a bit of a penny pincher and is always looking for a way to save a buck. But she means well."

Halley felt her face flush and heat creep up her neck into her ears.

"Really, I'm sure you just misunderstood her, if that is who you were hearing, anyways. Ms. Spark and I go way back."

"But what about your eyebrow? Why didn't Ms. Spark rescue you from the fire?" Halley stammered. She stood, but her feet felt like she had stepped in concrete and she was stuck firmly to the floor.

"Halley, listen." Ms. Mac stood and put her arm around Halley's shoulders. "This is an important lesson I want you to understand. When science falls into the wrong hands, it can be very dangerous. Yet when someone knows science and loves it, they can harness it in ways to help the world. When you apply science for the good, that is when the magic happens."

Ms. Mac walked around the room, going over to a wall of pictures hanging on a corkboard. "When I was a kid, I loved science, the messier the better. Kids are the best scientists because they don't have a filter that stops them from dreaming when they notice the world around them. This same science unites them so that they feel empowered and can band together if given the right opportunity. That is what this camp is all about."

"But why are you closing Camp Eureka then? Where are us kids going to go to band together and not feel so alone?" Halley was giving away everything, all her feelings. Did Ms. Mac know why Mom sent her to camp in the first place?

"When I was a kid, people wrote me off as being a silly girl despite asking me questions about how to fix things. And you, Halley Harper, also have that talent. A science knack if you will. Promise me this, I will figure out another way to keep kids enjoying science if you keep figuring out a way to enjoy science away from this camp."

It sounded like Ms. Mac was going to close the camp anyways. "But what is going to happen to Camp Eureka?" Halley studied the Einstein poster. Even his big brown eyes looked a bit sad when Halley spoke out loud the fate of camp.

"Right now, you should be thinking about your end-of-camp project to demonstrate to your parents the knowledge you've gained." The corners of Ms. Mac's mouth turned up into a smile and her eyes softened. "That is the best gift you can give to Camp Eureka's memory." She touched Halley on the shoulder, bringing her in for a hug.

Halley hugged Ms. Mac back, but her mind drifted to memories of her and Gracelyn laughing, to

Nathan playing archery, of being locked in the pantry, and the names signed near the Unbalanced Rock. If Ms. Mac didn't believe her that Ms. Spark was behind this, then she would have to take matters into her own hands and prove it herself. She wasn't going to let this camp end without a fight.

"Earth to Halley. Are you even listening?" Ms. Mac turned around to face her.

"Uh… yes… Thank you, Ms. Mac. I appreciate your help. I've got some work to do." Halley knew that she could figure a way around it. "Do you mind if we use some supplies in the pantry for our project?"

"By all means, help yourself." Ms. Mac opened her door.

Gracelyn and Nathan were standing there with questioning looks on their faces.

Ms. Mac closed the door softly.

"Well, what did she say?" Gracelyn blurted out.

"Ms. Mac doesn't believe me about what I overheard Ms. Spark say. We don't have much time. But I've got an idea." Halley grabbed both of their hands and started running towards the kitchen pantry. "I can't believe how much cornstarch there was."

"Oh come on, Halley." Gracelyn sighed. "What are we going to do with cornstarch?"

"Our end-of-camp project." Halley grinned, her eyes sparkling. "I think today we'll kill two birds with one stone!"

As they were running towards Pie Are Square and the pantry, Halley thought all about motion. It was what this camp session was about, right? The laws of motion got her into trouble, the laws of motion sent her to camp, and the laws of motion were going to be what saved Camp Eureka.

CHAPTER 19
THE CORNSTARCH PROJECT

THE PARENTS WERE COMING TO pick up the campers after lunch, so there was not much time to set up their project by the lake. Other campers had set up balloon rockets in the trees around the lake while others found toy rockets at the General Store to play with. Overall, everyone's project was getting things in motion.

A few campers came by asking questions. "What are you making?"

"It's a surprise," Gracelyn said, making the project sign.

"Are we going to get to try it?" they asked while Nathan finished making the frame that came up to his knees.

"What is that stuff you're pouring in there?" a few campers asked Halley as she dumped bags and bags of cornstarch inside the frame and carried water over from the lake.

"Don't worry. Everyone will be able to try it when our parents arrive." Halley finished mixing water and cornstarch inside the frame. If nothing else, it was going to be an epic way to end Camp Eureka. She wanted to make Ms. Mac proud.

Gracelyn taped the sign on a nearby tree when their project was complete.

Oobleck Walk-a-Thon
Can you cross without sinking?
Save Camp Eureka
$1/turn

When their pool of Oobleck was complete, Halley was the first to test it. She took her shoes off and took a running start. She ran ten steps across it before coming to the end. The campers looking on cheered, while a few parents started arriving.

Ms. Mac and Ms. Spark walked with a few parents as they arrived at the final camp activity.

Gracelyn turned to Halley. "I sure hope this works." Gracelyn spotted her mom and waved.

Halley nodded while staring at Ms. Spark. "Either it works, or I'm going to get in a lot of trouble." Halley didn't know if her mom was coming to get her or not, but for now she had her mind on one thing.

A loud whistle rang out interrupting Halley's thoughts, and she turned to see Ms. Mac step on the small stage getting everyone's attention. "Welcome, parents, to Camp Eureka Summer Set in Motion! I believe actions speak louder than words. Your campers have been busy learning all about Newton's Laws of Motion this week. They have completed their end-of-camp projects to show you all they've learned here at Camp Eureka. It has been my honor to witness such amazing kids and their creativity." Ms. Mac looked in Halley's direction. Her eyes sparkled like she was about to cry. "Enjoy learning science from your campers!"

Parents were hugging their kids and talking to them about their projects when Ms. Mac walked up to the Oobleck Walk-a-Thon. Halley's and Nathan's parents hadn't arrived yet. "Well, this looks amazing!" Ms. Mac turned to Halley. "I see you found the cornstarch in the pantry. Ms. Spark has got to see this."

Halley's stomach tightened, and her eyes felt like they were going to pop out. This was it. There was a big chance that this might not work, but Halley was willing to risk it.

"Come here and try this, Beverly!" Ms. Mac shouted as she took her shoes off. "May I try?" She backed up to take a flying leap and then said, "By the way, don't put this stuff down the drain. I learned the hard way."

Halley smiled.

"Woohoo!" Ms. Mac shouted as she took several steps light-footing it over the top of the Oobleck. "I did it! Isn't this awesome and very sweet to try and save the camp with your project!"

Ms. Spark walked up unamused.

Ms. Mac came back around to do the Oobleck Walk-a-Thon again.

"What a waste of money. Think of how expensive

119

all that cornstarch is!" Ms. Spark crossed her arms and looked down her nose at the Oobleck that was starting to get pine needles in it. "Besides, how are we going to clean this up?"

"Oh, come on. Live a little!" Ms. Mac insisted as a crowd of onlookers started forming. "Really, you've got to try this, Beverly. See if you can make it across!"

Ms. Spark narrowed her eyes at Halley.

"It will be amazing," Halley said in her most compelling voice.

"Just give it the old college try." Ms. Mac, amused, rubbed her missing eyebrow.

"Oh alright!" Ms. Spark carefully took off her glasses and her pristine white sneakers, showing even whiter feet. She poked one toe into the pool and slowly swung her other leg over.

"You've got to step lively!" Ms. Mac shouted, wiping her feet off in the grass.

"What?!" Ms. Spark squished her nose up. She slowly put her other foot in the Oobleck and immediately started sinking. She tripped and landed on her hands while the oozing Oobleck engulfed her. But the more she moved her hands and feet, the more she was stuck.

"I'm sinking!" Ms. Spark struggled as Ms. Mac walked towards her, giggling at the situation.

"I'm stuck, you fools!" Ms. Spark looked right at Halley. "Get me out of here, you twerp!" The more Ms. Spark struggled, the more she sank.

CHAPTER 20

TEAM COMET'S CONTRIBUTION

"It's Oobleck." Ms. Mac chuckled. "Calm down, Beverly. You should have run on top of it."

"You." Ms. Spark huffed, yanking her hand out of the Oobleck to point at Halley. "This was all your idea, you little brat!"

"Now, Beverly, just a minute. These are just kids!" Mac came over to help Spark out.

Halley stood motionless staring at how mad Ms. Spark looked. She was definitely madder than Mom ever looked. Halley said shakily, "I won't help you out." Then she took a deep breath and said, more confident than before, "Not until you confess to stealing money from Camp Eureka!"

"Halley Harper!" Ms. Mac's jaw dropped and her one eyebrow raised.

"Mac, get me outta here," Ms. Spark pleaded. "I can't believe we allowed this brat into camp. She's caused nothing but trouble the whole time she's been here." Ms. Spark tried to stand up and pull her leg out of the Oobleck. She was really stuck now. "Can't you see how these kids are just a waste of science? All they do is make a mess. I hate this camp. I hate these kids. I'm glad I took the money to use it on more useful scientific discoveries."

The parents gathered around to watch gasped.

Ms. Spark looked around. "What are you looking at, fools!? Get me outta here!" Her eyes bored into Halley. "I told you, girls don't belong at this camp. And I hate Oobleck!" Suddenly, Ms. Spark slipped and fell facedown into the Oobleck.

"Well, that girl—" Ms. Mac motioned to Halley— "just saved Camp Eureka."

A few parents helped pull Ms. Spark out.

"Come with me, Beverly. You have a lot of explaining to do." Ms. Mac grabbed Ms. Spark's clean elbow and marched her away to Energy Hall.

Gracelyn and Nathan stared at Halley with their eyes wide and jaws dropped.

Halley couldn't believe what just happened.

"You did it, Halley!" Gracelyn grabbed her hand and jumped up and down.

"We did it." Halley pulled Gracelyn and Nathan in for a hug.

For the rest of the afternoon, all the campers and teen counselors took turns running full blast across the pool of Oobleck. When Halley's dad and Ben came to pick up Halley, they took turns running across the Oobleck too!

"I can't wait to hear all about camp, Miss Disaster!"

Dad said, hugging her.

Team Comet collected quite a bit of money for the future sessions of Camp Eureka. In the end, no one wanted to leave because they were having so much fun enjoying the camp projects with their parents.

CHAPTER 21
THE RIDE HOME

HALLEY STARED OUT THE CAR window, lost in thought as they were driving home. She was glad Dad let her ride home with Gracelyn and Ms. Dee. Halley already missed camp and all the friends she made. She leaned her head back on the seat and listened to the soft music that Ms. Dee was playing on the radio. Halley peered over at Gracelyn who had fallen asleep, and Halley pulled Gracelyn's unicorn sleeping bag up around her.

A few stars were coming out in the twilight of the Texas sky.

Halley pushed the hair off her forehead and laughed when she found a bit of Oobleck caught in her ponytail. She closed her eyes and thought back to Camp Eureka and what she learned about Newton's Laws of Motion, her friends, and herself. She smiled when she thought about Nathan busting a water balloon on her a few days ago. Halley remembered getting high fives from the other campers and from Cameron thanking her for keeping Camp Eureka open. She wondered what was going to happen to Ms. Spark, but Halley was certain Ms. Spark would never be at camp again.

Then her hand drifted to the science kit sitting between her and Gracelyn. It was a take-home gift from Camp Eureka. It read: "Fizzy Fun Science Lab." Ms. Mac had leaned down and whispered as she handed it to Halley at the end of camp, "See you next summer, Halley Harper."

Mom might not let her open the kit, but she'd figure out a way to enjoy science anyway. She would say that she had to prepare for camp next summer. Until then, if she was a square peg in a round hole, she would just use science to redesign the hole. Halley turned her head up to the clear Texas sky just in time to see a shooting star.

HALLEY HARPER: SCIENCE GIRL EXTRAORDINAIRE
BOOK 2 PREVIEW

Halley raced up the sidewalk and stopped in front of the haunted mansion. The air smelled like a mixture of cinnamon sticks, candy corn, and dried autumn leaves. Halley adjusted her white lab coat, green safety goggles, and red backpack. She smoothed her tangled ponytail with one hand and clutched a giant beaker in the other.

She climbed the steps leading up to the mansion and noticed cobwebs stretched over the bushes. A cloud passed over the big autumn moon. Black bats hanging from the trees whipped about in the cool breeze. She shivered and was glad her Halloween costume involved a coat.

Jack-o'-lanterns glowed on the porch. Skeletons sat in chairs holding a sign that read, "Enter at your own risk." Eerie purple, orange, and green lights danced around, and she could hear ghostly noises inside.

Halley hesitated before going in. She didn't like haunted houses with things that jumped out and scared her. Taking a deep breath, she pressed the doorbell and braced herself.

Ding-dong.

An evil laugh cackled all around her. The skeleton's teeth chattered, and a figure floated behind the glass front door.

"What's the secret password?" the figure cried out.

"The secret password? Um, trick or treat?" Halley gulped.

The doorknob slowly turned, and a unicorn horn poked out of the door. A girl with a purple glittery face squealed and leaped out to hug Halley.

"Gracelyn," Halley shouted relieved, "I love your Halloween costume! I should have guessed you'd be a unicorn!"

"Do you like it?" Gracelyn beamed, adjusting the horn on her headband. "And of course you are a scientist!"

"At your service." Halley curtsied, holding her lab coat out to the side like a dress.

"Ooh! Is that for the experiment you're going to do?" Gracelyn touched the giant beaker. "Hurry, come on in! We've been waiting for you!" Gracelyn turned around and Halley saw a purple and pink unicorn tail pinned to the back of Gracelyn's pants. Her hair was in a French braid down her back, ending in a big white bow.

"Your mom is so creative!" Halley admired Gracelyn's costume and her house that had been transformed into a haunted mansion.

"Hi, Halley!" Someone with a green face, dressed all in black, and wearing a giant pointy hat sang out from the kitchen. She stirred a giant metal bowl that was bubbling. "Would you like a bit of my witch's brew?"

"Nice touch, Ms. Dee! Is that dry ice?" Halley admired the purple potion, putting her giant beaker on the kitchen table.

"I thought I'd try out a bit of science myself this year!" Ms. Dee beamed. "Thank you for agreeing to do some mad science for our haunted mansion!" Ms. Dee handed Halley the purple brew and adjusted the fake wart on her nose.

"Have you tried this experiment before?" Gracelyn said skeptically. "We don't need any disasters at the haunted mansion." Gracelyn elbowed Halley, smiling.

"I've tried it at my grandma's house before. She gave me everything I need to do Monster Toothpaste! I just need a bit of dry yeast. Do you have some?" Halley took her backpack off and peered inside, checking her ingredients.

"Of course! Gracelyn, show Halley where we set up the Mad Science Lab. The kids will be coming in soon. I'll bring you the yeast." Ms. Dee hurried into the pantry.

Gracelyn skipped, leading the way through the haunted mansion. They stepped out into the garage decorated like a mad science lab. Fake hands, eyeballs, and brains were floating in jars. A life size Frankenstein stood in the corner. Skeletons hung on metal frames, smiling like they were waiting to watch an experiment. A glow-in-the-dark sign taped to a table said, "Monster Toothpaste Station."

"You are going to love this!" Halley giggled, unpacking her backpack on the station table. "It really made an oozy explosion at my grandma's house!"

"Did you say explosion?" Gracelyn questioned. "No one is losing an eyebrow tonight, are they?" Gracelyn covered her eyebrows and stuck her tongue out, making a silly face.

"Not today! This is going to be super fun, you'll see!" Halley smiled and thought back to Camp Eureka.

What was Ms. Mac, the zany camp co-director, doing on Halloween? She remembered it was her turn to write back her friend Nathan, who she'd met there. She would ask him what his Halloween costume was this year.

"Here's the yeast!" Ms. Dee opened the garage door and tossed the yellow packets to the girls. "I'll check on you a bit later. I've got to let some guests in."

"What is the yeast for, anyways?" Gracelyn jumped up and down with excitement. "Are we going to make bread too?"

"Nope. Grandma said it's the catalyst!" Halley set up the supplies from her backpack.

"Did you say cat with a lisp?" Gracelyn grinned. "How is your cat, anyways?"

"Atom the Cat is awesome, but now is not the time to talk cats or catalysts. We don't have much time." Halley motioned to the kids piling into the Mad Science lab. "Here, safety first." Halley tossed Gracelyn the safety goggles.

Halley grinned. This was the first unicorn she'd ever seen with safety glasses on. Kids moved around, watching what the girls were doing.

The girls stood behind the table while Halley poured her grandma's hydrogen peroxide into the beaker. She passed Gracelyn a bottle of dish soap. "Put a few squirts of soap into the beaker while I mix the yeast and water."

"By the way, what makes this Monster Toothpaste?" Gracelyn asked as she squirted the soap into the beaker.

"Well, when we add the yeast it will look like

someone is squeezing a giant tube of toothpaste out. I'm adding some food coloring to make it fun." Halley squeezed the drops in, and a spooky green color dispersed like an alien hand swishing around in the hydrogen peroxide.

Kids who had formed around the station pounded their fists on the table while chanting, "Monster. Toothpaste. Monster. Toothpaste."

Excitement sparked like electricity in the air, and Halley wiped her sweaty hands on her lab coat. She hoped this worked the way it did at Grandma's house.

"What are you waiting for? The crowd is getting anxious." Gracelyn tapped her fingers on the table.

Halley picked up the yeast and water mixture. Her hand was shaking a bit. Then she quickly dumped it in the hydrogen peroxide.

The green liquid started foaming.

Halley blinked.

Suddenly, green foam shot violently out of the beaker. A few kids gasped and jumped away from the table. Gracelyn screamed as Monster Toothpaste blasted up into the air, hitting the ceiling before raining down.

The green foam landed on Halley's head and oozed down her forehead. She wiped off her safety goggles and looked around. The Monster Toothpaste, splattered all over the mad science lab, started smoking…

Hey y'all! Ask your parents to check out
SheLovesScience.com and sign up for the newsletter
so you can find out when the next Halley Harper book
is available. You won't want to miss it!

While you wait, you can check out my Instagram
@HalleyHarper and #HalleyChecksitOut

Last but not least, ask your parents if you can
leave an Amazon review of this book so that other kids
just like you can find me, Halley Harper, Science Girl
Extraordinaire!

ACKNOWLEDGMENTS

Writing a novel can be a long journey but I wanted to thank these people who made the trip unforgettable. I could not have finished this book without my husband and best friend, Matt. I still remember his grin at Pie Are Square and how he captured my heart from the very beginning. Thank you for encouraging me to keep writing when I wanted to stop. Thank you for the endless hours of talking about Halley over ice cream when our own children went to bed. And thank you for always believing in my dreams.

Thank you to my oldest daughter, Allie, for being the first to read Halley Harper. I loved reading this novel aloud to you and watching your expressions. Thank you to my son Andrew who is always excited to do science with his mommy. And thank you to my youngest daughter, Avery, who always wanted to get up in my lap to help me. You three will always be my inspiration.

Thank you to my mom who listened to my novel ideas from the start. I love that you have always believed in me from the beginning. Thank you to my dad who instilled excellence in me and to this day still calls me Miss Aster Disaster.

I am grateful to my friend and editor, Jennifer Vander Klipp, who taught me the art of writing fiction. It is surprisingly logical for this linear thinker! To my illustrator, Mel Cordan, who brought the vision of Halley out of my head and drew her on paper. I love that you have also been to a science camp!

Thank you to the kindred spirits that have drifted into my life, and I'll forever be grateful to you. Thank you, Megan C., who made potions with me; Catherine B. for telling me her camp stories, Morgan M. for inviting me to the zoo to talk shop; Amy R. for always remembering to ask me about how Halley was doing; and Amy S., you are my favorite Gutsy Girl.

Thank you to my readers at She Loves Science. You were the first to ask about a science book for kids and helped me decide it was time the world needed Halley Harper.

And to my Savior, Jesus Christ, who helped me persevere through this writing journey and continues to remind me that I'm writing books to help others, and that, truly, is what life is all about.

ABOUT THE AUTHOR

TRACY BORGMEYER is a chemical engineer and founder of She Loves Science. She lives with her husband and three kids in the Woodlands, Texas. Her life's passion is writing and inspiring parents to bring a love of scientific discovery to their kids. You can find her blogging about her science adventures at SheLoves-Science.com. Her first book *She Loves Science: A Mother's Guide to Nurturing the Curiosity, Confidence, and Creativity of Her Daughter* was published in 2016.

She enjoys spending time with her family, writing, reading, and experimenting with recipes in the kitchen. She loves being outdoors fishing and hunting around her hometown of Victoria, Texas. She also enjoys cheering on the Fighting Texas Aggies.

Visit www.tracyborgmeyer.com for upcoming book releases. She'd love to hear from you at tracy@shelovesscience.com and connect on Facebook at https://www.facebook.com/shelovesscience/

GLOSSARY

Friction—the resistance of motion of one object to another object.

Halley's Comet—a comet made of dust, ice, and gas that can be seen every seventy-five years from Earth. It was last seen in 1986 and will return in 2061.

Inertia—an object at rest tends to stay at rest; an object in motion tends to stay in motion.

Kinetic energy—the energy of objects in motion.

Lefty loosey; righty tighty—a way to remember how to loosen or tighten a screw; twist left (counter clockwise) to loosen, twist right (clockwise) to tighten.

Non-Newtonian fluid—a fluid that acts like a liquid *and* a solid depending on the force applied to it.

Newton's cradle—a toy made of balls suspended inside a frame that demonstrates Newton's Third Law of Motion.

Newton's First Law of Motion—a law about inertia. An object at rest tends to stay at rest; an object in motion tends to stay in motion. When forces acting on an object are balanced, the object has no motion. When forces acting on an object are unbalanced, the object will move.

Newton's Second Law of Motion—the acceleration of an object depends on its mass and the force applied to it. (Also shown as Force = mass times acceleration or F=ma).

Newton's Third Law of Motion—for every action there is an equal and opposite reaction.

Oobleck—a fluid with cornstarch suspended in water. The name "Oobleck" was given to this suspension after the book *Bartholomew and the Oobleck* by Dr. Seuss.

Potential energy—the energy stored in an object because of gravity based on its position.

Sir Isaac Newton—an English scientist and mathematician who, in 1687, published his theories about force and motion known as Newton's Laws of Motion. Legend has it that when an apple fell on young Isaac's head, it gave him the idea of the laws of gravity.

SCIENCE EXPERIMENTS IN
SUMMER SET IN MOTION

Oobleck

What you need:

2 cups of cornstarch, 1 cup of water, food coloring

How to make it:

1. Mix 2 cups of cornstarch with 1 cup of water

2. Add food coloring

3. Use hands to shape and pour mixture

What's the science?

Oobleck is a Non-Newtonian fluid, meaning it is a liquid and a solid. You can pour it and you can ball it up. It's sticky and it's smooth. When a force is applied it doesn't behave like a normal liquid. Other examples of Non-Newtonian fluids are ketchup, toothpaste, and shampoo. See more ways to play with Oobleck at www.SheLovesScience.com/oobleck

WARNING: Do not put Oobleck down the sink drain. It will cause it to clog up and may even get you sent to Camp Eureka! Dump the Oobleck directly into the trashcan.

Balloon Rocket Race

What you need:

String, a balloon, a straw (cut in half), tape

How to do it:

1. Thread the string through the straw.

2. Tie off both ends of the string to a doorknob and a chair.

3. Blow up the balloon and hold the open end shut.

4. Carefully tape the balloon to the string.

5. Move the balloon to one of the ends of the string.

6. Let go and observe how the air in the balloon pushes the balloon forward.

What's the science?

The air pressure inside the balloon is balanced when the balloon is closed. When the balloon is opened, the pressure inside the balloon is forced out. The forces are then unbalanced causing the balloon to shoot forward. It is an example of Newton's Third Law of Motion: for every action there is an equal but opposite reaction. See a video of this experiment at www.SheLovesScience.com/balloonrocketrace

Made in the USA
Middletown, DE
26 May 2020

96120315R00083